"NURSE, I AM SHOCKED BY YOUR CONDUCT—

I am going to have you replaced on this case as soon as possible!"

Trudy stood dumbfounded as the handsome young doctor gave the charges against her—deserting her patient, refusing first aid to an injured person, giving unauthorized and dangerous treatment. . . .

She knew they were lies—spread by the spoiled debutante who hated her . . . but how could she defend herself?

NURSE BETRAYED

Jeanne J. Bowman

PRESTIGE BOOKS
NEW YORK, NEW YORK

Prestige Books, Inc.
18 East 41st Street, New York, New York 10017

© Copyright 1966 by Arcadia House

All Rights Reserved

Printed in the United States of America

1

IT WAS the quiet hour at Dane Memorial Hospital. Visitors had departed; nursing shifts had changed; dinner trays were not yet being carried through corridors to reluctant recipients.

Two young doctors turned from the register to start their respective rounds, then stopped short. A nurse had rounded a corner, seeing neither, and had all but walked over them.

"Balloon tires," stated Dr. Erskine.

"Balloon soles," Dr. Kern corrected him. "Not a bad idea in their profession. Now if I could obtain a patent on air-filled shoe soles, I might be able to buy a slice of your mountain."

"Wouldn't work. Consider the patients. Nurse steps on pin. Blowout. Patient jerks; rips stitches."

"Or a slow puncture. Hiss. Patient unable to identify source, and an anxiety neurosis is triggered."

"And consider the necessity of installing a patch and pressure system. Long line of nurses waiting their turn to have their soles—hey, who started this?"

Kern looked after the departing figure of the nurse. "One of you, who is she?"

"Holmes, special. Gertrude, called Trudy. Not bad-looking, but neither this nor that. Hair," he elucidated.

"That's comforting, but I assumed her cap—"

"I meant," came the didactic retort, "it was neither one color nor another. Good nurse, though. Been on the Malda Morse surgery. Discharged as of tomorrow.

Mrs. Morse, that is. If she'd bleach it, take these TV commercials seriously—"

Dr. Jason Lee Kern closed both eyes. Malda Morse, wife of Dr. Malcom Morse, was the father of Pamela, about whose hair color there could be no doubt. It was red. And Pamela's friend, Karen something or other, was indubitably bleached; that is, platinum.

Well, one thing about being exposed to Erskine's mind and vocabulary: it kept one's own agile.

Trudy, with her neither-this-nor-that hair, went blissfully on. It was about to happen, the long awaited realization of a dream: a vacation with pay!

And all she had to do to earn it was to stand guard over Mrs. Morse at the fabulous Morse Lodge on Medicine Mountain; see that none of Malda's well meaning friends reached her. Or if they did, let her uniform, and if necessary concentration on her watch or some other equally professional gesture, send them on their way.

Dr. Garth Palmer had performed the surgery, a benign tumor. But Dr. Morse insisted that pressure had been secondary. What his wife really needed was major surgery on philanthropic projects, time to recover from excess activity, to build up reserve strength and possibly have "some sense drummed into her."

"Should have been a man with a dozen companies under her supervision," he had rumbled to Trudy. "She has executive ability. Everyone knows when she takes over anything, it will become a success. Nor will she take the glory."

Trudy had her own general conception as to what type of therapy would be needed. Isolation might be a part of it. But isolation with nothing to occupy an active mind could pop her right back into Memorial Hospital with the nervous breakdown the enforced rest had delayed.

"Now what can I dredge up—"

"Hi, Trudy; hear you struck pay dirt."

Happily she waved at the nurses clustered around one table, then methodically filled her tray. Peculiar; she had reached the cafeteria without being aware of

The Nurse on Medicine Mountain 7

it. Oh, yes, she had decided to dine there to save wear and tear before she packed.

"Trudy," one nurse asked as she squeezed in among them, "why do they call it Medicine Mountain?"

Trudy looked vague, then brightened. "Considering its location, I imagine some *shaman* performed *hyas tamanous*. Oh, all right; some Indian medicine man performed such healing it was called great magic. And he lived there, so the mountain—"

"Became the hide-out of modern medicine men? But not for the cure. For recreation, they say."

"Umhum. It has everything in season; fishing, hunting, skiing and perhaps rest from such arduous work. But I didn't know there were other medics there."

"Dr. Erskine has a lodge," offered one nurse.

Trudy nodded. That brittle young IBM was practically engaged to Pamela, the Morses' daughter.

"And Dr. Tom Whalen, though I understand his place is just a one-room cabin."

They named others until Trudy quipped, "What? No hospital, with that staff in residence?"

Trudy left before the staff nurses had rested away their free hour. Naturally, their talk switched to her.

"Why Trudy for the plum?" pondered one. "Oh, I know she's a good nurse, but Mrs. Morse doesn't actually need the best. A paid companion, or a relative, or even her daughter—"

"You'd better take a course in resort entertaining," an older nurse advised. "Having Trudy means not having a family; no one will be dropping in to take advantage of lush surroundings. Her friends are all nurses, and catch us flitting in on top brass, expecting food, shelter and entertainment."

"What—no boy friend?"

"I doubt it. She's been too busy paying her training and living costs back to the family doctor who staked her."

Trudy was thinking of "Old Doc Cowels" at that moment. She had garaged her car, patted the fenders, then reached in to load her arms with boxes.

Doc, the car and these clothes were paid for, and she

had money in the bank. Her mind flashed back to the tragic hour when she had awakened to the realization she was alone, not yet through high school, and without money to see her through and into a profession.

She had been with the Cowels at the time. They had refused to let her return to the dreary housekeeping rooms her mother's long illness had driven them to call home.

"Trudy," Mrs. Cowels had been brisk, "the doctor is going to ask a favor of you. I trust you will accept. He needs it much more than you do."

Yet even then she had not been able to believe he had any right to his feeling of guilt, "not known enough soon enough."

He had felt more at ease and, as she progressed, happier. In a sense they had become a family to her, except when their own were home, with grandchildren usurping any rights she might have assumed.

Interesting how his retirement and move to a warmer state had coincided with her graduation from training school. In a sense it had given her the freedom to build a life completely her own. However, thus far she hadn't found time.

But after this vacation she'd "put herself" in the hands of someone to be made over. Physically, that is. She was so weary of others saying, "You could be very pretty if you'd just do something." But no two could ever agree on what.

A two-hour drive and four hours in which to make it, she thought the next morning on starting out.

Dr. Morse would bring the patient out later in the day. The housekeeper would have everything ready, except for the small touches she, Trudy, would add to remind Malda Morse she was still a patient.

For the first hour she had no choice of driving time or speed. She was on a freeway. Eventually came the turn-off she sought, and she headed east through farm lands, with crops in, every visible energy directed to wintering homes and stock.

Above this land, like a rim, arose the mountains, deep purple against the challenge of towering grey white clouds. Well, the Morse Lodge was equipped with amusements for dull days. Dull days would be welcome after the last few years. Imagine having one's feet up before a roaring hearth fire and a good book in one's hand. Luxury.

She drove more slowly now that she was entering the foothills. Shaggy trees, most of their glory piled in gold and scarlet around their roots, had a few leaves left on to flaunt defiance.

She had a glimpse of a snow-covered peak.

"Ridiculous," stated Nurse Trudy. But there had been two doctors in the Dane Memorial corridor. One was Dr. Erskine and the other that new one. What was his name, and why had he been laughing?

"At me!" she cried aloud. "Why?"

Had there been anything at all wrong any place, the nurses at the café would have been quick to tell her. And why had she not thought of this before?

"Because," her voice was a little weary, "you are letting down for the first time in six years."

A hump in the foreground diverted her attention from herself. Hump? It was a mountain. But it wasn't clothed thickly with pine and fir, or even cedar. It looked like a mammoth bald head rimmed with thick black hair, for here the forests had made inroads.

Lava deposit, she reasoned as the sun peered out for a moment to turn the sharp sides of the rocks vivid.

"Medicine Mountain," a sign alerted her as she drove into a settlement. Methodically her gaze registered a post office, several hotels in between-season somnolence, stores, gas stations, a few obviously summer homes, and then a group of small homes which must belong to natives. They were city cottages, completely out of place in that background, yet comfortable in appearance.

Trudy stopped at a gas station, "just in case," and talked to the attendant.

"You take that bridge over there to the left—" he pointed in the general direction—"then start climbing.

No, the road peters out before it hits the summit; you take the only turn-off there is. Left again.

"Figure Miz Alpin, the housekeeper, will be lookin' for you."

Trudy drove across a rustic bridge with rattling boards and glanced down, thinking vaguely the river looked like a child compared to the mother stream she had sped along beside on the freeway. She climbed, using that one peak as a sentinel, then came to other lower ranges touched with snow looking like cup cakes dipped in powdered sugar.

Imagine even this change of climate within such a short range. It was later in the year than she had realized.

There was the turn-off, the dip, and down on the fringe of the bald spot, log lodges, cabins, car shelters, a veritable settlement.

Trudy turned into the largest grounds to be rewarded with an openwork wooden sign confirming her choice.

She pulled in beside a terrace, and promptly a door opened and a woman stepped out.

Now, thought Trudy, she really knew what "rawboned" meant. The woman was tall, not thin but without an ounce of superfluous flesh, and vibrantly alive. Her hair was brown, as were her eyes, and when she smiled Trudy knew she had never sat in a dentist's chair.

"I'm Miz Alpin," she announced. "You're the nurse woman? Girl, that is?"

Trudy met her searching gaze and said she was, and Mrs. Alpin nodded. "Mighta known Doc'd send out someone with common sense. Give you a hand with your bags; then we'll eat."

Giving a hand seemed to mean she stacked everything, then started off, carrying the load with ease and leaving little for Trudy. And Trudy walked along in her wake, slightly bewildered, feeling she had made a friend and something more, signed some pact with the woman.

They didn't go into the main room but through a

The Nurse on Medicine Mountain 11

door that led to a secondary staircase which had Trudy puffing a little as they reached the top.

"Higher up," stated Mrs. Alpin, explaining her short breath, "but we'll have you livin' again in no time. 'Nemic," she added.

Higher up? 'Nemic? Oh, of course. Higher altitude did make one breathless until one adjusted, and she'd been sending her car up three to four thousand feet from the valley. 'Nemic meant anemic. So she had a slight iron deficiency. Who didn't in the western part of the state, where drinking water came from snow fields untouched by mineral-bearing rock?

Mmm, lovely, she mused as they came out on a balcony or gallery running in a wide U above the living room.

"Now here's the doctor's wife's room, and here is yourn. Want I should hang things for you?"

Trudy said she had better; then she would remember where they were. Mrs. Alpin nodded, looked at her, then raised her eyes as she removed her hat.

"Steeped tea rinse," she stated, and took off, saying to follow the steps down; she'd be setting up the food.

Trudy gave the room barely a glance. It had windows looking out on a superlative view of small mountains. It had a small fireplace and big chairs and a nice springy bed. But Mrs. Alpin was more interesting.

Except that she's going to keep me mentally hopping to understand her, Trudy concluded.

Ready to go below, she stepped into the adjoining room and stopped short. What a peculiar odor. Not unpleasant, yet why would Mrs. Morse's room seem saturated with it? There were no urns or vases filled with anything to identify it. For that matter, the only thought association triggered by Trudy's sense of smell was the Sunday roast beef of her childhood.

Bay leaves, she thought, but could find none.

She was ready to pose a question when she entered the small dinette in Mrs. Alpin's quarters, but the housekeeper spoke first. "Orange pekoe," she announced, and Trudy backed off a little, for the woman was staring at her hair.

She sat down as ordered. She scanned the dishes placed before her, then lifted her head. This was pure old-time Oregon, from smoked salmon to huckleberry pie.

"It's delicious," she protested later, "but I can't eat another bite." Well, yes, she looked doubtfully at some snaky blue-black squares; she could take them to her room. Then she sniffed.

"Taseem," announced Mrs. Alpin, "You need it."

"Salal berries!" cried Trudy. "But I never thought of making anything of them."

"Indians did. Made a paste and dried it. Kept them a-goin' come bad weather."

But taseem? Oh, potassium. Of course, it seemed to come from any deep purple fruit or berry.

"Did the Indians teach you this?"

"Nope; my book did. Raised me four husbands on that book." And as Trudy batted her eyes, "First got took by artillery in the first World War. Second I cured of a lot o' things. Made him too strong. He tried to outsmart a tree. Tree won. Third was a puny one, but I built him up. Then he got to readin' about 'three times and out' and figured to quit bein' my husband so's he wouldn't get himself killed. Took off; ain't seen hide nor hair o' him since so I deevorced him and picked a good fourth. Fine man."

The shrilling of the telephone stopped a further dissertation on husbands. In a moment Mrs. Alpin was back.

"That was Doc Morse. Emergency. Gettin' a late start. You are not to worry. Now then, got you some good shoes? Time to go scoutin' the mountain so's you won't get lost if you go out alone."

Trudy had provided for this possibility and soon changed to ankle boots and an enveloping coat. But when she reached Mrs. Alpin, something else was added—a knitted cap the woman promptly pulled down over her ears.

"Cold wind off the peak," she explained, stared at

Trudy and nodded. "Get you a husband in no time, if we follow the book."

Trudy sputtered a little and found it useless. Mrs. Alpin was striding along, and what breath Trudy had left was needed elsewhere. And the mountain was beautiful. There were gaps where other worlds, delicately shrouded in blue mist, held an ethereal quality; and there were trails: cougar trails; bear trails. And in one evil-smelling, cup-like cave was a spring: sulphur.

"Better hike home now," her guide said, and started back at the same pace.

Nearing the settlement, she paused. "Looks like Tommy's got him some company," she said. "I'd better cook up."

Tommy? Trudy bowed to hide her laughter. Dr. Tom Whalen's dignity had just gone down the mountain.

But it wasn't Dr. Whalen who came out of the log cabin. A man in a heavy plaid jacket and coonskin cap took one look, then raced for his car and returned with both hands filled.

"This," he extended a package to Trudy, "is for you." And he again rushed to the car.

"I swan," murmured Mrs. Alpin, "the man's in love with you. Handed you a gift with his left hand, his heart hand, just like the book says."

2

TRUDY barely heard the man call, "I'll bring the rest up." For this man was the one in the Dane Memorial Hospital corridor who had laughed at her.

In love with her? Because he'd handed her a package with his left hand?

"Come on; hurry," muttered Mrs. Alpin. "Got to see what he brung you."

It was shaped like a box of candy, long and rather flat and still in a drugstore sack. Trudy stumbled along almost as rapidly as Mrs. Alpin, who finally came to a halt at the lodge kitchen table, then stood back to await the uncovering of the gift.

Carefully Trudy pulled out the box, frowned, lifted the lid and then her voice. "It's a hot water bottle," she cried.

"Now if that ain't thoughtful!" mused the woman. "Power goes off up here in a storm, but he brung you what'll keep your toes cozy if it does. Now as I see it, he's telling you he has a warm heart."

"Mrs. Alpin," the starch in the nurse was back, "a note here from the hospital says this is Mrs. Morse's toe warmer."

Then for no particular reason the two were in each other's arms, laughing hysterically.

"If you will tell me where to put these," came a taut voice, "I may join you in your hysteria."

They unwound themselves and looked at the newcomer, now minus the coonskin cap, his black hair standing up in drake's tails, his cheeks scarlet.

The Nurse on Medicine Mountain 15

Mrs. Alpin was equal to the occasion. "We thought the young man that's been tryin' so hard to win Nurse Trudy had sent her some candy. Couldn't wait to get our hands on it. And dogged if it weren't a hot water bottle."

"But not from him," Trudy broke in quickly, "or for me."

His expression, a pained smile, intimated he could see some humor in the situation, but not hysteria.

"Dr. Morse," he informed them, "said I was to hand this to the nurse so it would not be overlooked or misplaced. It seems his wife—"

"Has an allergy, she believes, to rubber," Trudy supplemented.

"Well now," soothed Mrs. Alpin, "I'll quick knit a cover so tight she won't know is it rubber or metal. You two take the gear up to the missus' room whilst I run up a pot of coffee. Like huckleberry pie, or maybe apple?"

The "gear" was divided, and the two proceeded up the back stairway, that being closest.

"I," came rather breathlessly from the man as they topped the rise, "am Dr. Jason Lee Kern." Then he gave a sharp bark.

"Altitude," murmured the nurse in Trudy. Swiftly she said, "Yes, Dr. Kern. I had heard you'd joined the Dane staff. In receiving?"

"Sea level to five thousand feet. Oxygen intake would assist. Yes, receiving. And how long does it take to recapture your breathing rhythm?"

"I assume that is an individual matter. I gasped the first trip up those stairs, then lunched, then went on a compulsory walk with Mrs. Alpin. She doesn't crawl. Most interesting person."

Dr. Kern laughed, and the change was amazing. "I've heard of her. Erskine calls her the witch doctor. Dangerous for the unsuspecting."

Remembering protocol, Trudy made her remark a question. "Do you think Dr. Morse would retain her services if she were a—" she faltered, remembering the left hand, the heart hand, and, cheeks scarlet, concluded—"threat?"

Dr. Kern looked at her, frowned and said, "I wish you would remove that atrocity you're wearing on your head. Your face—well, I would say you have a temperature."

So that was what she was running, Trudy thought, half hysterical again. But Mrs. Alpin had made her promise to keep it on until the doctor left. Why?

"Coffee's on," came a bellow from below.

Both jumped. "You go on," Trudy pleaded. "After the lunch she fed me, I couldn't take another bite."

"I could. I should have stopped for lunch." He hesitated, lifted his head and said, "What is the peculiar odor in this room?"

"Roast beef, Sunday," came Trudy's inane rejoinder. And she fled to her own room, longing to beat her stocking-capped head on the stone mantel. Now he'd add delirium to temperature, and she'd be thrown off her case before it started.

A tap at the door, and a laughing voice said, "Meaning bay leaf? Good thinking." And then booted feet trotted downstairs with alacrity.

Trudy waited impatiently. Dr. Kern had said Dr. and Mrs. Morse would not be up until evening. The "gear" he had brought up, he reported, consisted of "afterthoughts."

Unpacking it, Trudy shook her head. Canvas board and oils; number painting. Malda Morse would go quietly mad if she had to sit in one spot, eyes focused on matching numbers and colors.

Small boxes. Each contained something to be made from their contents: plant holders, match boxes, ash trays. That man didn't know his wife.

She saw Dr. Kern, hair sleeked back now, riding briskly back to the Whalen cabin, then saw smoke shoot up from the chimney like Indian signal writing.

"Now then—" Trudy wheeled; Mrs. Alpin stood there—"outa them clothes and into a kimono."

"But—" sputtered Trudy.

She said no more. Her clothes were coming off the

top of her head, and when she was able to reassemble arms, neck and limbs, she was being thrust into a warm corduroy robe.

"Hair," the housekeeper explained.

"You are *not* going to dye it?"

"Heaven forbid. Ain't a quicker way to bald a woman. But remember this. Does someone use something that takes the hair out, you buy you some strong yellow onions, slice them, then rub the juice into your scalp, heavy. Second husband grew him a fine crop of fuzz before he met up with that tree.

"Course," she had Trudy over the washbasin, rubbing in what smelled like naphtha soap, "does keep other folks away from you. But worth it. Onions, I mean."

She talked steadily as she massaged Trudy's scalp. "Time was folks figured dyeing hair made them insane. Kept on doing it, though. Some of them had special receipts. Made a paste o' lime and litharge, then added boilin' water till it was mustard thick, then rubbed this on the head and went to bed, rags tied round to save the pillows. Come morning, they had them a hard cap they had to rinse out."

Trudy, coming up breathless from the final rinse, cried, "Where do you get such information?"

"My book. Tells how everything should and shouldn't be done. Down now." And Trudy's head went down under the strong palm of Mrs. Alpin.

Something new was being added. Tea? She opened an eye. Tea that was so steeped it was copper color.

"That," she cried, "is tannic acid."

"Drink it, don't you? Don't hurt your stomach, won't hurt your head. There now. I'll just put some crimps in where waves should ought to lie."

Trudy let out a long breath. She had to see this through. Mrs. Morse had ordered, "Treat her well; she is very valuable to us."

She would treat her well, but her head would most certainly have another scrubbing once the housekeeper had retired.

The housekeeper wasn't retiring. She had built a hearth fire, pulled up a "turn-around rockin' chair" and planted Trudy in it firmly. She was to rest, sleep if she could. She, Mrs. Alpin, would be in often to turn her around.

Trudy risked one out-of-the-chair glance in a mirror. She saw nothing startling—except her reflection, that is. Mrs. Alpin had "did her hair in rags," and she looked more like a witch than the housekeeper was purported to be.

"Oh, yes." Back in her chair, Trudy nodded. Before metal and plastic curlers came in, women with curly hair did align the curls on rags. But if she rewashed her hair, how could she do the same?

Well—she rocked a little in warm contentment—if Dr. Kern had laughed at her in the corridor of Dane Memorial, he'd hoot the next time he saw her. And how long was he off duty? Would he be coming in for dinner tomorrow?

If she had any free time after her patient's immediate arrival, she would take a walk down by the Whalen cabin and maybe sprain an ankle.

"To be honest," she informed a log that was sputtering, trying to get up enough wind to bloom into a flame, "I'd rather have him holding my hand than my foot. And I might be replaced if I developed a limp."

She wondered drowsily when the Morses would arrive at the lodge and what would be expected of her that evening. Mrs. Morse would be in no mood to retire early, not after having had to wait for her husband all day. She fiercely resented being made to wait for anyone, as did all nervous patients.

"Two-handed bridge," she murmured.

"Give her one of my sleep drinks," a voice whispered.

"Miz Alpin, you shouldn't."

"Miz Morse, you know Doc said they were inoctupus."

"Innocuous, yes, and—"

"Look at her."

"Why, she looks beautiful."

"Give that young doctor one, too. Shoulda seen

The Nurse on Medicine Mountain 19

him sniff. But he was tied up in bow knots. Bet he ain't now. Give him a double."

Bow knots. Of course, her hair was in rag curlers. Trudy reached up both hands, but whatever lay on her head was soft. She opened her eyes. Mrs. Morse was beaming down at her.

"Have a good rest, dear?" Then quickly, "I've never seen your hair so lovely. Do look in the mirror."

Trudy's eyes were wide. Night had fallen darkly. An illuminated clock dial announced the hour. She had slept five hours. And here she was in a rumpled robe, while her patient looked brisk and anything but convalescent.

"Mrs. Morse," Trudy was on her feet, "you should not be up at this hour."

"But, Miss Holmes, I have been down all day. Now let us have a snack and find something to amuse ourselves for an hour or two."

They left, and Trudy fled to her bathroom to dash cold water on her hot face, then lift it and stare in the mirror. Her hair hadn't changed color. But it had "come alive."

Quickly she sprayed it, ran a comb through the waves, patted it and only then remembered to dry her face.

"Highlights," she murmured, "that's what that concoction of Mrs. Alpin's has given it."

Dressed, she went down to have Dr. Morse look up groggily. "Mountain air's doing you good, Nurse," he intoned. "More than I can say for Jake. He looks doped."

Trudy spun around. Dr. Jason Kern was slumped in a deep chair. "Altitude," he informed Trudy seriously.

"Housekeeper," chuckled Morse. "Come on, son; I'll walk you home."

Kern stood up. "Nurse looks better able than you, Dr. Morse. You need rest after today's debacle. Fact it," he squared his shoulders, "I feel fine. Excellent dinner, Mrs. Alpin."

"You doctors are like a lot o' people—so busy takin' care of the other fellow, tellin' him what to do, you don't follow your own do-its. I'll heat up," she told Trudy, and motioned to her to walk down to the other cabin.

They stepped into the sharp chill of the night; even the stars were seeking the momentary cover of cloud blankets. The scent of pine and fir and other scents Trudy couldn't identify made the air a heavy intoxicant.

"I don't need to walk," Dr. Kern assured Trudy as they started down the well lighted path, "but I am curious. I had that 'snack,' as she called it, early this afternoon, went to the cabin and passed out. Fire managed to stay alive, which I deduce means the housekeeper knew what would happen and came down to replenish it.

"I understand you too slept. The same way?"

Trudy nodded.

"Now don't say it was because of the change of altitude. Had we gone to a lower altitude, a warmer climate, that could have had some effect. In short, what did that incredible housekeeper slip into that 'snack'?"

"I don't know." She could answer that without violating relations with her patient. "But if she did, I would like the prescription."

Dr. Kern nodded. "Now to see if there are any side or aftereffects; then—" The word "then" was a threat. Or a hope?

They said good night. He smiled and said she looked like a different girl, and while she could have said he too was charged, it wouldn't have been a compliment.

But the air there was wonderful. It must be the air, she thought, tripping happily back to the lodge.

Dr. Morse was having dinner at a small table before the huge living room fireplace. Mrs. Alpin, he confided, would carry tray dinners to Mrs. Morse and herself.

"She said," he confided, wiping his curving lips with a napkin, "the only way to rest is to undress for it."

Trudy's laughter bubbled. Yet wasn't it true? Dining properly clothed, one who felt she had wasted too

The Nurse on Medicine Mountain 21

much time in bed would put off disrobing as long as possible.

"What do you think of her, Nurse?"

"She's wonderful. But how about this famous book of hers?"

"You should read it sometime. Make a new woman of you; not that you need renewing. Oh, all right, Mama; I'm sending her up."

But Trudy swung back to pick up her own tray and was told seriously that now Mrs. Morse was dis-dressed, she should have no trouble getting her to bed.

"No pills," Trudy warned.

"She don't need none. Her family always took a nap after Sunday dinner." This might have left Trudy groping had she not, at last, recognized the reason for the bay leaf odor.

A quick glance at her patient's tray was reassuring. Mashed potatoes, pureed peas, creamed chicken and gelatin. Yet, nearing Mrs. Morse's room, she felt she should hide her own with its fried chicken, baked potato, leaf salad, and apple pie with cheese melted over it.

Mrs. Morse had at no time been a difficult patient. At first she had hidden behind a wall of pain and fear; then, after surgery, she had maintained a wall of reserve.

Entering definitely behind the housekeeper with her swifter ascent, Trudy found all walls were leveled.

"Miz Alpin," she was protesting, "you know I can't abide mashed potatoes."

"Right now it's what kinda food can abide you that's important," came the retort. "Now eat up. Nurse here nearly starvin'." She whirled out, and Trudy looked at her patient. Then both laughed lightly.

"What do you really think of her?" Mrs. Morse asked, dipping into the tasteless white mass. Risking her displeasure to take her mind from her menu, Trudy told her of the hot water bottle episode.

In the next room, Dr. Morse, preparing for bed, nodded. He'd picked the right nurse. He hadn't heard Malda laugh like that for months.

"Just watch your cap." Mrs. Morse was now sputtering through the gelatin.

"My cap?" Trudy reached for her winged symbol.

"Have you never heard of 'setting your cap' for a particular man? She has. Over the left ear is a—she calls it—'come-on.' Right ear: 'Someone else reached me first.' Back of the head: 'Anyone is fair game'; and over the brow, 'Don't like men.' "

"But I wear mine—"

"Exactly." There was a delightful coo in the patient's voice. "Yours is always dead center. That is the 'You'll have to prove you're worth it' sign. And she won't stop at that."

"Meaning she'd slip the cap? Ah, but Mrs. Morse, how many men know the cap code?"

"Knowing my housekeeper," she retorted, "any she felt worthy of you would be briefed." And Trudy believed this was probable.

Trudy said she would take the trays down and save Mrs. Alpin the steps, and Mrs. Morse laughed and said she believed Miz Alpin had younger legs than she.

"Have! Left a bottle o' vinegar on her bedstand," announced that worthy. "Splash it on, cupped hand," she ordered Trudy then turned to Mrs. Morse. "Car just drove in."

She had no time to say more. Footsteps came racing up the main stairway; then a curly red head popped in the door.

"Pamela," said Mrs. Morse sharply, "you were not to come up for another week at least."

"I didn't," cried her daughter. "I mean I didn't drive. I mean, Karen came up, and she drove her car, and I just came with her as a chaperone."

"Chaperone?"

"Well, Mother, be reasonable. Karen heard that nice young Dr. Jake was weekending at Tom's cabin. She'd met him, and she says he was really quite up with her, so she wanted to—well—"

"Make hay?" suggested Mrs. Alpin.

"Well, sort of. I mean, have a place here, and I

asked Erskie, and he said we could use his lodge but—"

They waited.

"Well, Karen went straight down to Tom's cabin and knocked, and Dr. Jake opened the door, said, 'Oh, it's you,' and yawned in her face. Then he shut the door."

And only Trudy saw the look of complacency which spread like oil over the housekeeper's countenance.

3

DONNING her best professional manner, Trudy lifted her wrist and consulted her watch, "Mrs. Morse," she said in a cool voice, "I believe you would like to talk with your daughter alone. Shall we say for ten minutes?"

"There is really nothing to discuss," Mrs. Morse returned. "It is early enough for these girls to return home."

"But, Mother, we simply can't. And we can't stay in that awful big Erskie lodge all aone, and you do have extra rooms here, and—"

Trudy walked off reluctantly, bumping into a thoughtful Mrs. Alpin. "Half a mind to wake Doc. Put Mrs. Morse back a month, does that blonde come hikin' in. Always one to make a scene."

"But Dr. Morse has had such a difficult day. I imagine I could—"

"No, me. I'm the only one can better that girl."

"Mrs. Alpin," a cool voice sounded from the kitchen, "we were obliged to leave the city before dinner. You may prepare just a light meal for us. I see you have plenty."

Outraged, the housekeeper shot ahead to her own domain. "Out," she ordered. "What I fix up I take to the Erskine lodge. Do you want to eat, go there."

"I shall report you to Mrs. Morse immediately."

Trudy stepped forward. "I must ask you to leave my patient alone. She is here to recuperate from pressures of all kinds. If you wish, I will call Dr. Morse."

The Nurse on Medicine Mountain

Their eyes locked. Trudy saw only blonde hair and blazing indignation in pale blue eyes.

"No one," she informed Trudy, "tells me what I can or cannot do. Not in the home of a friend."

"Well, I can." A sleep-drugged Dr. Morse, wrapped in a robe, appeared. "I thought I told you young ones you were not to come near here until I gave the word. Why did you?"

"Pamela was worried about her mother."

A snort of derision sounded from Mrs. Alpin. "Then why did the two of you go down to the other cabin first?"

The blonde wheeled on her. "To check with Dr. Kern on Mrs. Morse's condition."

"Knowing I was here?"

Suddenly Karen was all smiles and dimples. "But, Doctor dear, we heard you had been delayed."

Dr. Morse reached for Trudy's wrist, read the time, then spoke to Mrs. Alpin.

"Call Dunbar. Tell him I want him to convey my daughter and her friend back to the city immediately!"

"Oh, but we are staying at Dr. Erskine's lodge."

"You may be. Pamela is not."

Now Trudy had time to study Karen, whose last name she had not yet learned. But then she was a nurse; introductions were sometimes overlooked.

She was older than Trudy had at first thought. The long hair just clearing her shoulders was deceiving. Once one had studied the face, one found it at variance with the coiffure. She was determined and confident because of her beauty.

"Very well, Doctor." She sighed. "I don't mind remaining in that big, cold—"

"Tain't cold," broke in Mrs. Alpin, "You had Dr. Erskine phone up hours ago. His man, down in the village, come right up and set the furnace goin' and brought up a passel of groceries. Got you a can opener, you can live there a week. That is—" she hesitated.

"Yes, Mrs. Alpin," urged Dr. Morse.

"Well sir, that old *shaman*, dead these hundred years, comes back 'long about this time. Had this tepee there where the Erskine lodge stands; sweat bath just 'longside where he stuck his patients. Some of 'em died there. They get to caterwaulin' nights like this."

"Hmm," muttered Dr. Morse. "Nurse, will you send my daughter down, then stand by until I come up. Sedative is indicated. Sorry. I had thought my wife would be given a few days before being molested."

Trudy sped away, hearing Karen's indignant, "Molested? Why, I never—"

She found Pamela in tears, Mrs. Morse pale and shaken, and swiftly sent the daughter on her way.

"Isn't it fortunate this happened so soon?" Trudy observed.

"Fortunate!"

"Umhum." Trudy rubbed a swab over the beaded brow and started steering her patient to the bed. "Now you won't be braced against such an occurrence. It happened at precisely the right time, with Dr. Morse present and Mrs. Alpin prepared." And soft laughter bubbled up from Trudy.

"Honestly, that girl!" sighed Mrs. Morse. "No, not Pamela; Karen Overseine. Her mother is so ineffectual she uses her to whip her very fine father into line. And of course she is so spoiled she only wants what seems impossible to have."

Trudy relaxed a little. That meant Dr. Jason Lee Kern had not yet succumbed to Karen's beauty.

Reflected head lamps flashed, and in a few moments Dr. Morse appeared.

"You can relax, Malda," he told his wife. "Dunbar is driving Pamela back. What Karen does, follow or precede or remain here, is up to her. But I doubt," his shoulders started shaking, "she will remain at the Erskine Lodge."

"Mother, we must have led a good life to deserve a woman like Miz Alpin."

Trudy left them alone for a moment. If she went to her window looking down on the Whalen cabin, she, as Mrs. Morse's special, naturally wanted to arm herself with knowledge of the activities of the blonde Karen.

The Nurse on Medicine Mountain 27

She was standing now in a veritable spotlight, one of several lighting the path between the lodge and the cabin. Trudy sighed. From there she looked like a snow nymph, silver white against the dull green of the trees.

Now she was tiptoeing toward the cabin, something in her hand. A note? There; she had tucked it under the door and was walking slowly back up and, thank goodness, to her car.

Assured the car was heading away from the Erskine Lodge, Trudy moved restlessly. After her long nap, she was not tired. Perhaps, she thought hopefully, she might help Mrs. Alpin. Not that the housekeeper would ever need help from anyone, yet—

"Spot o' coffee?" Mrs. Alpin greeted her. "Was just pourin' out. Need somethin' bitter to take the taste o' that girl outa my mouth.

"Don't think o' nobody but herself."

Trudy sank into a chair. "Perhaps she's never needed to, really, though I believe she does head a lot of charity drives."

"Heads," grunted Mrs. Alpin, "but never hands or foots them. Well, least I scared her out of overnighting at the Erskine—" She stopped as a buzz sounded.

A moment later she turned back from the telephone. "Beat me at that. She only took herself to a mo-tel." She stood a moment thoughtfully. "Half a mind to go down and swipe me that note she left the young doctor. Figure she told him to come down there to visit her."

"Maybe he'd enjoy that."

"Enjoy? That young fellow? So tired he don't know the meaning o' enjoyment. Hasn't had a vacation in years. Worked his way through without a let-up. Doc Morse, he figured he'd get him away somehow, to let down. Years o' work; then her."

"Her people are quite wealthy, aren't they?"

It took the housekeeper a moment to digest that, then she shook her head. From what she'd seen of "Dr. Jake," he wouldn't be one to sell out for an easy life.

"Seen? Then he's been up here before?"

"Nope. Bunch o' doctors from Dane's held a bull session on him in there." She nodded toward the big room. "One or the other had knowed him since he was knee-nigh. Then he come up yes'day mornin', and I looked him over. He fit."

"But you wouldn't—" Trudy put more feeling into her plea than she realized. Granted Mrs. Alpin might tip a nurse's cap to establish a romance barometer, she must know she could not go further.

"No, that'd be the same as stealin' a body's right to experience. But I wouldn't be beyond providin' an anty-tote."

Antidote? Trudy carried the thought to her room with her. She had asked if that had been contained in whatever she had given Dr. Kern and been told that "weren't nothin' but some henbane, him being interested in experimentin'."

Trudy had checked on her patient and was herself just slipping into bed when the word returned. "Henbane." Great goodness! Admitting it was one of the lesser members of the deadly nightshade family, it was still dangerous.

She slept fitfully with harrowing nightmares about standing by, hands bound by her oath to Mrs. Morse, while the housekeeper poured beakers of deadly poison into Karen.

A wan Trudy crept to the kitchen the next morning. "See there?" Mrs. Alpin was staring out the north window. "The anty-tote. Dr. Morse. Now Dr. Jake can call and tell her he's already got him an all-day date with a staff member."

Under the table to which she had taken her first cup of coffee, Trudy delivered a sharp rap of left foot to right ankle. Regardless of how she felt about Mrs. Alpin, she should have faith in Dr. Morse.

"Now then," Mrs. Alpin had swung away, "must fix them a lunch to carry them through. Bad weather comin'."

Trudy escaped to her patient's room to find her quite willing to spend the morning in bed, and worried over her desire.

"It's natural," Trudy assured her. "You resented re-

The Nurse on Medicine Mountain 29

maining in bed when it was enforced. Now you are free and can use it for relaxation. A good book?"

Mrs. Morse sighed. "I should take care of that mail. Such stacks of it. With the holidays not too far away, everyone will be needing to know if I can or cannot head some project."

Trudy grasped the opportunity, mentally. "As your daughter has taken care of all thank-you notes, perhaps I could list queries and write regrets."

There was a fretful protest at having to give up her duty as chairman of this or that committee when she would really be quite well by the time the work was under way. No, she really didn't want to, but it was her duty.

Lightly then Trudy tossed her dart, with laughter. "I am thinking of a patient who wondered if she would ever be asked to do anything worth-while. She had been a business girl, married into the upper echelons and was unable to explain to her husband why she was never invited to head anything and served only in the lowliest groups—she with her executive experience."

And now, if Mrs. Morse was comfortable, she would run down and see about breakfast. The housekeeper was enthralled with a cook-out lunch for the men.

Yes, Mrs. Alpin said, she'd be glad to have the nurse fix a tray. She herself wasn't one to cook up pap.

Trudy sniffed hungrily at the breakfast she was preparing for the two doctors. She heard their hearty laughter from the big room, where a mammoth fire now roared on the hearth, and wished she had just a little of Karen in her make-up. A Karen would find some excuse to intrude.

Placing the tray on the bed table, Trudy heard her patient give a sigh of pleasure. "Mrs. Alpin's bread," she explained. "You can't toast it crisp. Which kind is this?"

"Rice," Trudy replied, a note of doubt in her voice.

"Fine. One of the recipes from her book. You must browse through that book some day. I feel sure she'll consent, you not being one to ridicule."

"Ridicule?"

"One of Pamela's friends opened it to 'How to Win a Sweetheart,' then found next to that a recipe for 'Lemon Sponge' and after that, 'How to Kill Slugs.'"

But Trudy's mind had stopped on the first subject. How did one go about winning a sweetheart? Dimly she heard her patient describe the book, published in 1856 in New York by Dick and Fitzgerald and aptly titled, "Inquire Within," with the subtitle, "Anything You Want to Know," and listing over three thousand seven hundred facts.

"But think of the progress in the last one hundred years," Trudy protested.

"Granted, yet the principle remains the same. I thought of that when I viewed the God is Dead program on television. I wondered why no one refuted the claim with the simple explanation that the principle of mathematics, for instance, is not destroyed because a man-made computer malfunctions."

"Oh," Trudy nodded, "in the Book is related man's current concept of healing at that spot in time."

"And from that spot we have progressed in our understanding."

Maybe, thought Trudy, heading down to her own breakfast, just maybe. "How to Win a Sweetheart" had changed in format in the last one hundred and ten years, but if she could find the principle—

"Look at 'em," said Mrs. Alpin, pointing out to the two men heading uphill, light back packs jogging, "goin' out to weary their bones and rest their brains. Come night, they can both rest together, get rid o' the inside fight—"

"Conflict," interpreted Trudy, and decided at the rate her mind was whirling, she had better find a way to weary her bones.

"Oh-oh," Mrs. Alpin breathed, "like a cocklebur. Glad the men are out o' sight. Pick up your tray and scram to your room. I'm about to lie, and I don't like to get caught at it."

Trudy flew, but not out of hearing. She heard the protest of brakes, then Mrs. Alpin's reply to a question. "Went out to get them some time to talk without interruptions."

And no, they hadn't said where. Then she offered a contrary tidbit, "Men folk usually head for the stream. Easier walkin,' fishermen having beat them down a path."

By the time Trudy reached her room and looked down, Karen's silver-white rain boots were rapidly changing color. She was heading for the fishermen's path by a short cut.

"She'll be back." Mrs. Alpin appeared with the coffee maker. "Got the doors barred, but that won't keep her voice out. Could be you'd better swallow fast and get in to Miz Morse. I'll 'lert her so's she won't panic."

Trudy hesitated a moment, then conceded Mrs. Alpin was right. It was sharp sounds, sudden emergencies, that sent her blood pressure shooting skyward.

She relaxed when laughter sounded from the next room, and when she went in to find Mrs. Morse alone, the latter confided the reason.

"Mrs. Alpin says I am to 'pay no mind' if voices are raised below stairs. She is about to teach Karen a lesson on how to catch a husband, if she has to sit on her and give her a quiet-down pill."

Trudy shuddered a little. Yet how wise of Mrs. Alpin to put humor as an umbrella between the patient and the sound of an altercation. "My goodness, how—"

"To quote her limerick, 'You spoil your chances do you make advances.' Next the routine. You are allowed shy glances. Then when the man first speaks to you privately, you lower your eyelids and blush. But never allow him to believe you are won until the ring goes on the right finger of the left hand."

Trudy looked so concerned Mrs. Morse asked the reason. Trudy couldn't tell her that her own cheeks had been so scarlet Dr. Kern had thought she was running a temperature, so she qualified, "I was just trying to see Miz Alpin blushing."

The tray empty, the nurse took it to a hall table, then returned to find her patient looking at her thoughtfully. "I want to thank you for awakening me to how selfish I was about duty," she began. "I have taken on projects, chairmanships, committee work that I loathed, through a mistaken sense of duty. I have neglected my own life and family, and have deprived younger women of work they need."

She was now calling a six-month moratorium on all outside activity. She would immediately write a form letter to that effect. Then she wanted Trudy to take it to the village, where she would find a public stenographer to type the copies she would need.

"And, Trudy," she said when she had finished, "why not remain in the village for lunch? Your absence will deprive Karen of one more court of appeal. Now run and dress in something warm."

Half an hour later, Trudy was happily rumbling across the wooden bridge toward the settlement. This was more like the vacation with pay she had envisioned. Her patient was cozily tucked in with a good book and a stern guard at the door, and she herself was dressed in mufti any winter resort would approve. Even the brass buttons picked up the glimmer of her hair slipping out in curls beneath her velvet beret.

Everyone seemed so friendly. Of course Mrs. Alpin could have prepared the merchants by telephoning in orders she was to pick up, yet it was nice.

She browsed in the library, after turning the copy over to the public stenographer, then went to a tiny cafe and lunched sumptuously.

Maybe the weather was miserable—grey and black clouds, like dirty curtains, were hiding snow peaks; an icy wind whipped one's ankles and froze one's toes— but she felt wonderful.

She must visit here often, see it whirling with the colors of ski parties congregating after snowfall. She might even find time to learn to ski herself. She really must find some outlet of activity, not become a one-horse nurse.

It was a wonderful world, bursting with opportunities for self-development, from Orange Pekoe hair to— Trudy's thoughts stopped. A man had come from a small hardware store to hail her.

"Hey, miss, mind stopping in an' picking up a pane of glass? Seems some woman went crazy on Medicine Mountain and tried to bust in. Gave Miz Alpin quite a time. Now the dame's trying to get Miz Alpin arrested, and she's got the sheriff out lookin' for you for running away and leaving your patient alone."

Trudy froze; then her world exploded, falling in bits, a million whirling bits. Or was that snow?

"Here comes the deputy now."

4

THE bits continued to fall before her eyes and her mind. She, Gertrude Holmes, R.N., had failed in her duty. She had allowed a patient to dictate to her. She had not remained at the scene of battle.

"You Nurse Trudy?" A young man had come up to stand and push at bits of wet snow landing on his nose. "Dep'ty Sheriff Kline here. When you've loaded, I'll go ahead."

"But—"

"Mrs. Morse said I'd better."

"You talked to her, to Mrs. Morse?"

"Let's say she did the talking; that is, when she wasn't laughing."

"Laughing?" echoed Trudy, and relaxed a little. "Forever why?"

"Well, this woman who wanted in couldn't get in, so she wrote a note and tied it around a rock and aimed it at Mrs. Morse's window. It got in."

"Yes?" urged Trudy. For what was humorous about that?

"Well, Mrs. Morse wrote an answer, tied it around the rock and tossed it out the broken window. Her timing was perfect. The other one had just walked up and looked up. She has, I'm told, quite a shiner."

Karen with a black eye? Trudy's own grew large and, though she was unaware of it, beautiful.

"Miz Alpin wanted to doctor it, but she blew up. Should have let her. Makes a salve out of train oil, stone pitch, resin, beeswax and stale tallow. Smells to high heaven, but it sure takes the pain out."

They waited until the pane of glass was carefully tucked in on the rear seat; then the deputy went on, "She wants you to give her emergency treatment until the doctors return. Mrs. Morse doesn't want you to touch her or talk to her. That's where I come in. I'll drive on ahead."

Dutifully Trudy placed her car in alignment with the police car, then jumped half out of her seat as it took off with a howl of its siren. Well, she couldn't appreciate police protection from anyone more than from Karen Overseine. The less contact she had with her, the less Karen could misconstrue.

They made pretty good time until they reached the bridge; then the police car flashed a slowing signal, and Trudy looked far ahead. Across the exit, at an angle which blocked both lanes, was a silvery-white car. Karen's.

Karen was nowhere to be seen. However, she had underestimated the power of the law. Kline jumped out of his car, went to hers, found the keys in the ignition and swiftly swung the car around to drive it toward town.

"You go on," he ordered, slowing to call to Trudy. "I'll catch up with you as soon as I impound this vehicle and write a ticket. And don't stop." He backed again. "We know her down at headquarters."

Trudy nodded and drove on. Not that she would have stopped for her under any circumstances. Well, almost any. A nurse would naturally have to lend first aid in certain situations. But if Karen were well enough to cause as much trouble as she had—

Trudy braked. She allowed the windshield wipers another clearing half-arc. She hadn't dreamed it. A figure lay directly ahead, stiff, motionless and rapidly being blanketed by snow.

"Oh, no," objected Trudy, "she's been down only long enough for polka dots. Now how do I handle this? If I pick her up, I'll have to take her to the lodge, and once she gets in—"

The head swiveled. Naturally Karen must be wondering why anyone wouldn't come crying to her in her position.

"I know," mused Trudy, and let her car horn express her irritability. It worked. Karen geysered up out of the road and headed for the driver's side of Trudy's car. Once she was around the hood, Trudy started moving on.

She felt like an utter heel. Karen looked dreadful. Of course she had brought all of this on herself, but didn't everyone, in one way or another?

Behind, in the now rapidly falling snow, car head lamps gleamed. The deputy's car. There; it had stopped. Trudy slowed. Obviously he had picked up Karen, for he was backing to turn-out. He was, in short, taking her back to the village.

Swiftly Trudy continued, parked, jumped from the car and headed for the lodge, which seemed silent on the first floor. She scurried up the stairs and heard laughter; then she waited outside of Mrs. Morse's room to reassemble her nerves before she entered.

"Bring us a windowpane?" Mrs. Alpin greeted her.

"Did you see any sign of Karen?" asked Mrs. Morse.

"Yes to both." Trudy could smile. "I think Miss Overseine is in the village now."

"Did you talk to her? Did you treat her?" Mrs. Morse continued anxiously.

"No. She tried to stop me, but I was too concerned about you. And aside from a red and swollen eye, she seemed all right. I mean, had there been any type of concussion, she couldn't have moved so rapidly."

"Thank goodness," breathed Mrs. Morse. "And now you know why I sent you away. A most determined girl, Karen. Here." She handed Trudy a crumpled note, obviously the one tied about the rock Karen had hurled through the window.

"Sweet," Trudy read, "I am here to take over your correspondence. I will organize your holiday activities for you and contact the principals. Your housekeeper refuses to let me in."

"And," supplemented the patient, "the note I sent

back down, the one which floored her, said, 'All matters have been handled. Thank you for your offer; another time, perhaps.' "

Trudy nodded. That would have "floored her," for she would have used her own plan to establish herself at the lodge.

"Enemies," stated Mrs. Alpin, "are easier to deal with."

"For dinner, what?" Mrs. Morse inquired eagerly.

"Moose. Nurse here'll like it. Tastes same as mutton, only more so."

"Then I shall come down and dine with the men and the nurse," stated Mrs. Morse. "I feel so much better. Such a load off my mind," she explained. And Trudy knew she meant the threat of holiday overwork on projects.

Trudy went into her professional routine and found her patient was better. She herself felt immensely better when Mrs. Morse told her she was not to change. They were among friends. They would dine en famille.

A call from the deputy sheriff further relaxed them. Karen was heading west. She had refused treatment "before witnesses." And she and her car would run out of the snow belt within the hour.

Trudy turned, after relaying the message to her patient, to find her looking smug. "Nurse," she confessed, "I feel utterly uninhibited. I did not aim that rock; truly I didn't. But it did what I have been longing to do for years. It—"

"Clobbered?" offered Trudy.

"Wonderful word. It clobbered that spoiled girl."

Her patient intent upon having a nap, Trudy went to her room to relax for the first time within the hour. A big chair before a big window, and outside, fat flakes rapidly turning Medicine Mountain into a gigantic mound of beauty.

The four of them, Mrs. Morse, Mrs. Alpin, the deputy sheriff and herself, had scored a victory. But was it only temporary? And wouldn't Karen, who had disliked her before, now build up that dislike into hatred?

Mrs. Alpin came in to deposit a cup of hot chocolate

beside her. "It's the little snowflakes we ought to fear," she intoned. "These here big fat ones that make such a show—pouf, they go at the first off-sea breeze."

"Anything extra in this cup?" Trudy asked suspiciously.

"Nope," the housekeeper replied. "Figured after what we all been through today, don't need no extras. Lookit, men comin' back. Look good. If I weren't so keen on Tom Whalen as a proper husband, figure I'd work me up a charm on this one for you."

By the time Trudy had said, "Well, really!" the woman was gone.

The men did look ruddy, relaxed and happy, Trudy admitted. She smiled a little as they hovered on the edge of the timber and wondered if they were scanning the terrain for the white car.

Then Dr. Morse spotted the broken window, and they hurried forward.

Trudy could hear Mrs. Alpin explaining the cause, and, hovering close to a slightly opened door, hear her further remarks.

"Surgeon, ain't you?" Mrs. Alpin asked. "Way I figure it, don't take no more know-how to putty in a pane o' glass than it takes to sew back a stretch o' skin you done slit to get t' the inside."

"Doctor," that was Kern's voice, "I'll suture if you hold the patient—the ladder, that is."

"She would choose a second-story window," grumbled Dr. Morse. "Any other room, we'd wait for a man from the village. That girl!"

Trudy waited tensely for Dr. Morse's reception of the news she had left her patient. Then Mrs. Alpin came up, chuckling.

"Got 'em drinking coffee and eatin' doughnuts," she reported. "Coulda had my man come up and fix that window. Figured it'd be better for the doctor to have a first-hand taste of that Karen's back-handed wreckin'."

"I shouldn't have spent so much time in the village, or even allowed Mrs. Morse to send me."

"Doc don't think that way. Said it was right smart of Miz Morse to clear you out. Said Karen wouldn't nowise want a pretty nurse around and would've tried to run you off."

Trudy's sigh of relief was like the breeze which whipped around the corner of the lodge, lifting the spots, or snowflakes, to reveal a scene of fantasy beyond.

"Now take you a nap. Men plan to soon's they get the window in. Young Tom telephoned. He's comin' up; ought to be here time dinner's ready. Great one for moose."

Trudy leaned back. Of course. Dr. Morse had more faith in his housekeeper than in his nurse. And rightly, where the Karens of the world were concerned.

Then she straightened. Young Tom? Dr. Whalen was due there for dinner? Smiling, she relaxed again, her memory flashing back to her student days when Whalen had been an intern. There had been an epidemic of cardiac cases, not isolated, among the student nurses, herself included. That young Irishman had even made her forget her debt to Dr. Cowels. She'd spent good money for an off duty ensemble, hoping to impress him.

Suddenly she was on her feet. What would she wear to dinner? Imagine dining with two of the handsomest young unattached physicians on the Dane Memorial staff!

Ostentatiously she reached up and took herself by the ear, leading herself back to the easy chair. They wouldn't know she was present, any more than young Tom Whalen had known what she wore when she passed him in the corridor.

"All you need do, Trudy Holmes," she informed herself, "is listen with intelligence as they talk shop. And if you get any more wild ideas, I shall ask Miz Alpin for a strong dose of her lethal nap medicine."

Awakening from a short nap, Trudy went in to hear Mrs. Morse say, "Dear, don't change into uniform; you look lovely as you are."

Trudy had Mrs. Morse comfortably gowned in a flannel wrap-around when Dr. Morse came in from his nap and, excused, she went down to see if she could help Mrs. Alpin.

On the threshold of the kitchen, she paused. Mrs. Alpin was joyfully submitting to a bear hug from some young monster.

"And this," she said breathlessly when she was released, "is our girl."

Black-lashed blue eyes looked at her with anticipation but no recognition.

"Nurse Trudy Holmes," Mrs. Alpin began.

"You look wonderful, Nurse," Whalen said. "I didn't recognize you. This Medicine Mountain really has something, hasn't it?"

" 'Tain't got diplomacy," Mrs. Alpin interposed dryly. "Now you two young ones get in there and set the table."

Doctor and nurse stared at each other; then both burst out laughing. "Come on, Nurse," ordered the doctor. "I know where to find dishes, and you know where to put them. We'll make a good team."

"And you, Dr. Jake—" Mrs. Alpin was looking beyond them—"build up the fire. Want Miz Morse's back warm while she's eating. Digest better if she's warmed outside 's well as inside."

In the big room, the three looked at each other. "Isn't she wonderful?" Dr. Kern remarked.

"The very best," Whalen confirmed. "I only hope she never comes to me for surgery. She'd be sitting up telling me where to place the stitches. But then she's known me since I was a pup. In fact, she started my interest in medicine."

They worked as he talked, and Trudy listened, enthralled.

The Whalens had a cabin on the river just beyond the village when Tom was a boy. Always a victim of minor accidents because he couldn't "keep up with the gang," he would fall under Mrs. Alpin's ministrations.

"Then when we were back in the city and the family doctor took over, he'd be so baffled he'd blow. Made me curious. And I began looking for answers."

Dr. Kern straightened from placing a mammoth log

The Nurse on Medicine Mountain 41

in place. "Find any?" he asked. "Or learn what—" he nodded his head toward the kitchen—"she had or didn't have?"

Trudy stood cradling a vast yellow bowl filled with russet apples ("teeth whiteners, better'n toothpicks"). She was aware of the beauty of the big room, its warmth, the flickering fire casting light and shadow on the two momentarily earnest men.

"I'm still searching." He turned to Trudy. "What did she have you ingest to bring out such radiance?"

"Orange Pekoe tea," Trudy replied absently. Then quickly, "I mean well steeped. My head. Oh, dear, you have me confused."

"Better watch it. Can't have you too glamorous; we need you around Dane."

She and her ideas about intelligent listening!

She neither talked nor listened intelligently at dinner. The three medical men talked fishing with a little hunting thrown in. Before they were through, Trudy knew where to find rainbow trout, how to anticipate a smelt run and, as a postgraduate tidbit, how to choose fish from market, this contributed by Mrs. Alpin.

"Look at their eyes," she warned. " 'Be they not clear, inward distress can result.' "

"There's the book again," chuckled Dr. Whalen. "But remember that, Nurse. I'll bail you out if you're arrested for demanding to look a fish in the eye when marketing."

" 'Immature minds,' " quoted Mrs. Alpin, " 'betray their possessors by mouth.' " But she laughed as she spoke, then whisked back to her domain.

Trudy offered to help, but no help was needed. Mrs. Alpin had a system: out of the dining room into the dishwasher, course by course.

After "bread pudding, elegant, with hard sauce," the men escorted Mrs. Morse to what they called the "ski lift"—a swing chair lifting to the gallery and making a climb unnecessary—then returned to the fire for coffee.

Wistfully Trudy looked down. So much for Orange Pekoe glamour. They had not suggested she return after preparing her patient for the night. But some day, she promised herself grimly, even though it took Mrs. Alpin's book to do it, she would evoke a different response.

Mrs. Alpin and her ridiculous idea about choosing either doctor for her. Neither knew she was more than a pair of hands protruding from a uniform.

Early the next morning, she heard two cars give goodbye honks and knew the men were heading for some ski bowl over the eastern range where they would be assured of packed snow. They would return to Dane Memorial without stopping at the lodge.

Dr. Morse, on night call that evening, left in midafternoon, and the Morse Lodge slid into silence. It was restful, no doubt.

Mrs. Morse napped, read and became reacquainted with the radio. Trudy napped, tried to read and spent considerable time on short walks, though now the paths were sodden with melting snow.

Imagine weeks like this. And what about her patient? She must find something of absorbing interest to tide her over this quiet convalescence.

Trudy stopped in the back hall to remove her galoshes and heard Mrs. Alpin grunt, "Oh-oh. Nurse, come quick. Out there. You go to the door. I break out in a rash when I talk to him."

A car had slid in, and from it was emerging Dr. Erskine. Brisk, alert, he headed for the house and, Trudy noticed, the front door. Her lips quivered a little, wondering if he too broke out in a rash on encountering Mrs. Alpin.

"Oh," he spoke abruptly, "outside, Nurse. I want to talk to you. I am shocked and dismayed by your conduct on this case. I shall ask for a replacement as soon as I reach the city. Well, what have you to say?"

5

TRUDY smothered a provocative reply and substituted a query. If Dr. Erskine would tell her the charges, she might be able to explain.

Not that she wanted to. She would much rather ask him what right he had to ask for a replacement, this not being his case.

But there was protocol to observe, if she were ever to special at Dane again.

Briskly he gave the charges. She had deserted a patient in time of need. Fraternized with questionable characters during her hours off duty. Refused first aid to an injured person.

"Aiding and abetting; that is," he coughed, "condoning the therapy of an unqualified person."

Behind his back they sometimes called him Dr. I.B.M. She might tell him his computer had been fed the wrong material. If she dared, she might even call his diagnosis wrong. But alas, he was a doctor and she only a nurse. And where with another doctor she might have joked a little, she could not with Dr. Erskine.

"I fear this glamorizing you have been undergoing has gone to your head," he concluded.

Where else? she wondered hysterically. Imagine an Orange Pekoe binge.

"You mean, I suppose," she ventured, "that having had a few days of rest, the first in a number of years, I appear to look better. But, Dr. Erskine, you have known me since my student days. Are these charges in character?"

He debated, even as she wondered how she could prevent him from carrying this story to Dr. Morse, his future father-in-law? For wasn't that part of a nurse's duty: to maintain friendly relationships wherever possible?

"No," he conceded after a moment. "I had to assume you had been imbibing some of that witch doctor's brew. You don't seem surprised," he added suspiciously.

Now she could smile. "I imagine it is a matter of viewpoint. I was on an errand for my patient when word came another had attempted to invade her privacy. I avoided first aid because there was a police car just behind, ready to render any aid necessary. Dr. Morse approved."

"Morse did? Hm. I'll look in on Mrs. Morse; you may remain downstairs until called."

"Yes, Doctor," she agreed. What else? Dr. Morse would have asked Erskine to "look in on" his wife out of courtesy to the younger doctor if for no other reason. And he was purportedly to be their son-in-law. Poor Pamela.

A very chastened Dr. Erskine came downstairs some time later. He gave Trudy a nod which could have meant anything, and had reached and was out of the door before she could show him equal courtesy.

As soon as his car had turned toward his lodge, Mrs. Morse rang. Trudy, hurrying up, found her patient with flushed cheeks and accelerated breathing.

"Dr. Erskine and I had a slight argument," Mrs. Morse explained. "He felt I needed a companion here and suggested one with whom I am not compatible.

"I informed him you were the ideal companion. You knew when to leave me alone, which was more than others did. But the unmitigated nerve—" she panted.

What could she say to offset this? Trudy dredged deep. "I imagine even brighter men than Dr. Erskine have been brainwashed."

"Brainwashed?"

"I've seen lots of men say yes when they were cornered by a determined woman, haven't you? Yes to

The Nurse on Medicine Mountain   45

get away? Can't you just see him trying to back up a wall and finally agreeing to save himself from future encounters?"

The vision of dignified Dr. Erskine trying to scale a wall backwards sufficed, and soon Mrs. Morse was laughing a little. Yet her real concern, Trudy knew, was having a son-in-law who could take a Karen seriously. What a team those two would make!

"He's one of the most conscientious—" Trudy began.

"Anatomically speaking," agreed Mrs. Morse. "Ah, well, in time he'll mature. He may even learn something about women, and Karen and Pamela learn more about men."

"Maybe," quipped Trudy, "he should read the book."

"Mrs. Alpin would burn her treasure before she would allow him to touch it." But she was laughing and relaxing.

"It should be preserved," Trudy ventured. "Too bad there isn't someone she could trust to copy and classify it." And having dropped the seed, she went on to her own room.

Deliberately she went to a window she had seldom used. The view was not inspiring. It looked up on the Erskine Lodge; from that vantage point a rear view.

Now why was Erskine there at this time? Trudy knew the Dane Memorial schedule. He was off schedule. And Erskine was never off anywhere, from his sleek brown hair to the precise set of his eyeglasses.

It was more than curiosity that sent her downstairs to find Mrs. Alpin, her neck at an awkward angle, surveying the same scene.

"Brought him a man out from town," she said over her shoulder. "Up to somethin'."

"Maybe he's planning a rest, a short vacation."

"That man? He's too scared to take a rest."

"What is he," she chose the other's term, "scared of?"

"Not knowing all the answers before the questions have been thought up. Got to know 'em, right or wrong. Can't let nobody think he don't know everything. Poor guy."

Trudy shook her head. She had heard Erskine called many things, but never a poor guy. Just what had she heard on the few cases she had specialed under his severe jurisdiction?

She smiled a little, remembering one patient who had sworn the doctor didn't dress in clothes but in a capsule. Another had said she felt she was a laboratory specimen rather than a human being.

"Compensation," Trudy deduced. And seeing Mrs. Alpin's bewilderment, "He's trying to make up for being so young by acting too old."

"Hmph, Dr. Jake and Tommy are younger 'n he. They're people, spite of bein' right good doctors. Thought I heard the buzz."

She had, and flew off upstairs, for it was a call to her rather than Trudy.

In a few moments she returned, stumbling a little and going directly to the wooden range kept in the big kitchen against such time as a power failure occurred.

"Fireproof," she explained as she opened the oven door and drew from it a book: the book.

"Here—" she thrust it at Trudy—"you hold it whilst I fix a tray. Nurse," she beamed down at her, "ain't nothin' I can do for you for this here idee. Coulda put it in a safe down to the city bank, but I needed it to hand. And I've feared night and day some scalawag would get his or her hands on it and ruin it for all time."

Trudy's bewilderment showed, and swiftly Mrs. Alpin explained. "Miz Morse said she should ought to class and copy; make up a dozen or so small books so's a body wouldn't have to thumb through lookin' for a hurry cure or maybe a recipe."

Trudy looked down at the book, not a vast tome but a normal novel format. It had a dull blue cover with gilt inscription. Idly she opened it and read three consecutive paragraph titles. "The Art of Being Agreeable." "Destruction of Rats." "Almond Pudding and Sauce."

She opened to another section to find: "Baldness." "To Destroy Ants." "Breach of Promise of Marriage."

A glance at the top of the pages, and she found

The Nurse on Medicine Mountain 47

there the epigrams Mrs. Alpin was so fond of quoting, such as the one: "Take things always by the smooth handle."

Well, she relaxed a little, if Mrs. Morse were sincere about this project, she had a good year's work cut out for herself.

Her eyes had been caught by a title: "To Ascertain Whether a Bed be Aired," and the nurse in her read, "Introduce a glass goblet between the sheets for a minute or two. . . . If the bed be dry, there will be only a slight cloudy appearance on the glass, but if not, the dampness will assume the more formidable appearance of drops, warning of danger."

Couldn't she see the nurses at Dane or any other hospital rushing along, goblets in hand, to tuck them into bed with their patients?

"Mind me the one meal Dr. Erskine had here." Mrs. Alpin was busy slipping "custardy cakes" on to a small plate. "He was eatin' right good; then he asked what. I told him it was beef bubble and squeak. Like to not get out the front door. Never ate here again."

After the housekeeper departed with the tray, Trudy checked the recipe. No more than previously roasted meat, sliced and fried, and cabbage "cooked in two waters," warmed in the grease and added.

"Interesting," mused Trudy. "Now had she called it London Broil or A la Deutsch—something tells me he's a label thinker. And he doesn't know cooking labels."

Now how would Dr. Kern or Dr. Whalen have reacted? Dr. Tommy, and she must watch herself on labels there. Dr. Whalen would have inherited the taste and label from his British forebears. And Dr. Kern?

"Guinea pig," she deduced. "He'd have enjoyed it and demanded the recipe."

Trudy enjoyed the "custardy cakes" and coffee, her respect for Dr. Morse mounting. His housekeeper might have unusual terms for her cooking (and her procedures), but he knew his wife's lagging appetite would be tempted, even as he knew her privacy had a better chance to be inviolate.

Or did he? Trudy swept up as a car drove in. She

watched. A woman got out, and the man turned, shouting a few words. The woman waved, then, picking up an overnight bag, advanced toward the house, even as the man drove out.

Trudy was nearly swept over by Mrs. Alpin as both headed toward the door.

"Get up to your patient," muttered the housekeeper. "Let me handle this one, or we're stuck for the weekend."

Trudy closed her eyes. Weekend? This being midweek, that would be quite a visit.

"Figure he got him a special doe license an' is takin' off to see can he get her. Won't be back till he does."

From the balcony but out of sight, Trudy listened to the word battle, as much as she could hear of it.

"But, Mrs. Alpin, you can't leave me out in the cold on this mountain. It isn't as though I could call a cab."

"I kin," the housekeeper told her grimly, "and they's motels down to the village. Could be the inn's opened, too."

"Oh, dear, and I didn't come prepared. Well, I'll just run up and sit with Malda until you find me a place to stay. And don't forget, you must assure my credit."

"Sorry, ma'am. Dr. Morse said, 'No visitors.' You can wait up at the Erskine Lodge. He's there."

"I most certainly will, and I'll demand that he telephone Dr. Morse and report your treatment."

"You do that."

Trudy hurried in to find Mrs. Morse stiff with apprehension. "Did she?" she began.

Trudy nodded. "She's phoning for a cab to take the visitor to a motel, after she's located a vacancy. Meanwhile, your visitor is en route to the Erskine Lodge."

"Oh, dear," sighed Mrs. Morse, then brightened. "I do believe it will be all right. He had her for three weeks one summer."

Then she looked ashamed. "Please forgive me for speaking this way. She's a wonderful woman, and I really can't blame Cal for getting rid—I mean, for finding a place for her to stay when he's on one of his trips. She is so—well, intense."

"That you tense up with her?"

"Well, yes. Yet she is so fine, so vital. She fixes you with her eyes—I mean she holds your attention, and you feel she has you under her thumb and you can't get away. Nurse, what am I telling you?"

Trudy thought: the truth. Instead she said lightly, "Wonder what the book has to say about tensions and tenseness."

"Oh, fun. Yes, do let's look."

They could find neither tense nor tension in the index and had about decided these conditions had not been paramount a hundred years ago. Then Trudy thought of hysterics and solemnly reported one should "avoid excitement and tight lacing."

"Try nerves."

"Nervousness," corrected Trudy. " 'Cheerful Society,' early rising, exercise in the open air, particularly on horseback, and No. 15. Avoid excitement, study, and late meals."

Under Prescription 15 she found a mixture of camphor and ammoniated valerian, and realized that was another member of the nightshade family. But couldn't it be compared to the barbiturates of this day, fatal only in an overdose?

Mrs. Alpin came in to report she had telephoned Dr. Erskine and told him she had acted under the orders of Dr. Morse. "Like I told him, let in one, you let in all, or feelin's get hurt. He grumbled till I told him I'd called for a car and got her a place at a motel. One of the far ones, so's she can't walk it too easy. Then he said Dr. Morse had used his usual wisdom."

Trudy nodded. He had when he'd brought his wife to Mrs. Alpin. And now, relaxed, she was happily intent upon the project of copying the book.

Trudy had to go to the village. She would need paper, a brace of pens, and some notebooks. Later she would arrange to have her findings typed.

"I took typing in high school," Trudy ventured. "It would be better to keep this within the family, wouldn't it?"

"Then I shall call the doctor and have him bring a typewriter. Trudy, you are an answer to my needs. Miz Alpin, what are we having for our evening meal?"

Soberly Mrs. Alpin shook her head. "Nothin' too good to celebrate such a time. Did I think you could stand it, I'd give puffed pie with wow-wow sauce."

At Trudy's gasp, she turned to her. "It's hot, and it's got everything from mustard to catsup, and vinegar and pickles. First taste you say, Wow—"

Hurriedly Trudy said she doubted their patient was quite equal to such a regimen. Mrs. Alpin readily agreed. But she'd "think up something special."

When she left, Mrs. Morse decided to start her project with food recipes. "Then I can be forewarned."

She explained that heretofore the Morses had not spent consecutive weeks at the lodge; no more than three at a time. And they had always come from the city laden with food, rather dictating their menus.

"Yet we found her contributions enjoyable; sometimes surprising, but always edible. My interest in the recipes are their basics, which might be important if one were isolated over a period of time."

She had opened the book and now read absently, "Suffer the miller to remove from the flour only the coarse flake bran." She stopped, laughed, said first one had to find a miller to suffer, then asked if Trudy minded going to the village.

Trudy did and didn't. Her last trip had been fraught with worry; needless worry, she reminded herself. This trip she might even enjoy.

The skies were putting on a spectacular as she drove off, but the roads were clear of snow and fairly well drained of slush. She glanced up at the Erskine Lodge as she passed and saw someone polishing a window. Not Dr. Erskine. Yet why this sudden refurbishing of the lodge? Interesting.

She learned part of the answer in the general store while listening to two local women talk as they picked out birthday cards for some mutual friend.

"Who, me? Cook up there? I'll say not. Why, that

The Nurse on Medicine Mountain   51

woman is so full of aches and pains, if she ever woke up feeling good, she'd think she was dead and gone to her just reward."

A muffled question, and a voice, like a shrug of the shoulders, "Who knows? Maybe she's worn out all the old doctors. Needs 'em young and ignorant. Not that Erskine is ignorant, but he's serious-like."

Trudy picked up paper pads, clip board, pencils, pens and the rest of the miscellany on Mrs. Morse's list, but not before she heard the last words.

"Ought to turn Miz Alpin loose on her; she'd cure or kill her, one or the other."

Trudy smiled at the chuckle in the woman's voice and went on. At least one mystery was solved. Dr. Erskine was either bringing or sending a patient out to his lodge. She wondered if a nurse would accompany her and if it would chance to be one of her many friends at Dane.

Then she became interested in the air and the sky. The air was brittle, the sky a rhapsody in color, gold and scarlet and purple against an ice blue background. Winter was definitely on the way in.

She found the housekeeper in a brown mood. "Better git out your red flannels," she warned.

"You mean you don't like snow? You living here on this mountain?"

"I like it, but I don't like folks with no brains cuddlin' up to the mountain, time like what's comin'. That Dr. Erskine's really up against it. Even phoned me for help. Did I know anyone he could get in to cook and housekeep for Miz Overseine and her daughter Karen. The Miz's sick. Karen wants to hide out till her black eye's gone. Seems she can't explain it to folks. Figure I know why."

So did Trudy. Perhaps too many had longed to blacken one, even as had Mrs. Morse, but had restrained themselves.

Then she awakened. Imagine this beautiful Medicine Mountain with Karen on the hill above, forever a threat to her patient and to her own peace of mind.

6

NURSE Trudy Holmes drew a deep breath and placed a question. "Does the patient know?"

Mrs. Alpin shook her head. "Couldn't raise me the gumption to tell her, least not till I figured me a way to rid the mountain of the girl."

Trudy tried to lighten her gloom. "What did you tell me about the big fat snowflakes?"

"These here are little fine, driftin' snow that sifts into a freeze. They'll be housepartyin' with girls, leastwise till her eye gets better-lookin'. And they'll be runnin' down to borry this and that, Dr. Erskine havin' him just a bachelor place.

"Then there's the mother, sick-like. Be callin' on you when a doctor ain't around, and you go to her, and *she*'ll sidle in, and once she gets herself in, she roots."

Trudy nodded. Something had to be done before that snow drifted in to freeze. To appeal to Karen or her mother would be useless. Nor would Dr. Erskine act for her.

Suddenly she snapped her fingers. "I've got it. I am calling Dr. Morse to lay down the law to Erskine." She glanced at her watch. "I might catch him at Dane now. You hold Mrs. Morse's attention so she won't come in on the extension."

Trudy prefaced her call to Dr. Morse, once she had reached the Dane Memorial Hospital switchboard, with a caution. Her call was not an emergency affecting Mrs. Morse's health, yet it was an emergency in another field.

The Nurse on Medicine Mountain   53

At that, the doctor sounded a little breathless when he responded.

"A threat to her peace of mind," Trudy said hastily, and explained what was happening on Medicine Mountain. "I felt you could convince Dr. Erskine, his house guests were not to trespass here, and he in turn convince them."

"So that's whom the young idiot leased to," groaned Morse. "I doubt he identified them in time to refuse. Good thinking, Nurse; I'll get in touch immediately. And I am now giving you a strict order. You are to allow no one to visit the wife without my written permission, understand?"

"Definitely, Doctor, but does that apply to medical men?"

"Well, no, just the female of the species." He hesitated a moment, then said, "Mrs. Morse telephoned me earlier on another matter. I am having the typewriter sent up. I think you have hit upon something that will hold her attention."

If given a chance, Trudy thought, going up to her patient. She nodded cheerfully at Mrs. Alpin, who scurried out of the room.

"What on earth is the matter with her?" Mrs. Morse asked. "I've never before seen her look defeated."

"I'm not sure. Would your precious book have any prescription for ridding one's surroundings of unwanted people? I have just talked to Dr. Morse. I called him. You might call it preventative therapy." And then she had to laugh.

"Can you imagine Dr. Erskine leasing his lodge, then, after the deed was done, learning he'd leased to Mrs. Overseine?"

"Oh, no," cried Mrs. Morse. "Oh, the poor lad. No wonder he seemed so upset this morning. But what about your call to doctor?"

"Neither Mrs. Alpin nor I would be able to convince him, as could Dr. Morse, that he was to 'lay down the law' to his tenants that they were not to drop in here without permission from him."

Mrs. Morse leaned back. "You are a nurse, Trudy, in

the true sense of the word. So much wiser to prevent than to attempt to cure a situation once it has developed. Now do go and ease Miz Alpin's mind. For some reason she can't cope with Karen."

Trudy doubted even Karen could cope with Karen, but she tried.

Dolefully the housekeeper shook her head. "Gives punch to my hit, do I have to strike her like," she conceded. "But she'll sift in. You watch. Mother can't tell her own child she don't want to see her. Pamela will be Karen's first guest."

"Not with her father alerted," Trudy prophesied, and Mrs. Alpin brightened.

"But I still feel in my bones I got a come-uppance with that one ahead."

The celebration supper was not as the housekeeper had planned. It was handicapped by the dietary restrictions still imposed on Mrs. Morse, and clouded by the threat of a Karen within shouting distance.

Yet Trudy found it delicious. Potato scones were deep fried to golden brown, then surprisingly revealed they were one half minced meat. She eyed the "yarb salad" apprehensively, for who knew what herbs Mrs. Alpin had used? They proved to be merely chopped watercress, parsley and a few touches of rosemary, oregano and savory, barely enough to start the taster questioning.

Dessert, too, was a compromise. Mrs. Alpin confessed she got "that upset" she let a sheet cake burn, but burn sliced off. The rest, cut up, had been immersed in a creamy custard.

"I'd planned such an up and comin' vacation for you," she told Mrs. Morse.

"Break that word down," came the rejoinder. "I have vacated the scene of my earlier difficulties. Any new ones will be a change, at least."

Trudy took that thought to her room with her later. Vacation to her had meant having a rather riotous time. Not that she had had such a time since childhood, but she had heard others relate their experiences and occasionally, from a distance, had seen adults playing like carefree children.

Well, she was certainly having a vacation from her usual routine, and it could be a gay time except for— She jumped as the soft buzz sounded and went in to find her patient looking thoughtfully amused.

"Trudy," she confided, "I have isolated the cause of our housekeeper's gloom. She doesn't fear anything Karen might do to her. She does fear Karen will ruin her chance of marrying you off to a nice young man."

"But I—" sputtered Trudy.

"I know you are not shopping for one. I told her no Karen could run off a man who really loved you. And she told me," Mrs. Morse paused to laugh, "Karen was the kind to see that none would be allowed near enough to you to learn what a lovable person you are."

Their laughter dispelled the tension of the day, and both slept well, to awaken to gloomy skies.

"Canvas bags," Mrs. Alpin observed. Then, seeing Trudy's eyebrows rise. "Mean canvas holds more longer, but once it lets go, snow comes down in buckets."

"Is that bad?"

"Could be with women who're used to other folks leapin' to their whistle. Snow don't leap to any whistle. Trap them women folk in, and who knows?"

Trudy nodded. She had had patients held to their beds who fought inactivity frantically, automatically insuring they would have to remain longer. Being snow-bound or bed-bound or even house-bound, she thought, called for inner resources.

Mrs. Morse came equipped, or almost.

"Trudy," she began as she entered to check on her, "we need an old dictionary and a cook book that translates weights into amounts. This recipe specifies drams. Now I know a dram is an eighth of an ounce, but what housewife carries a scale in the kitchen?

"And this, 'a faggot' of herbs. Oh, and this in a recipe called Half-Pay Pudding, an economical Christmas pudding. 'Take the weight of two eggs and a half in their shells, of flour.' Would you mind driving to the village?"

She would enjoy it. And yes, her car had snow tires. And yes, she would take her time and pick up any other reference books she saw which Mrs. Morse might need.

"However," she warned, "don't expect an answer to: 'Boil sufficient rice.'"

Happily she went on her way, wondering how one could take the weight of two and a half eggs when eggs were of different weight? She trusted the prescriptions in the book were more explicit.

Another gloomy day, she thought, driving off, yet it was beautiful. She glanced at the carport of the Erskine garage. No silver white car was yet there.

And now the snow began, and she instinctively started to chart the road. A narrow single lane and, once over the barren spot, trees thrust heavy arms as though to impede the car.

A thicket seemed to dissolve before her; then reproachful eyes stared at her, and what she had thought to be a stump and twigs bounded away. Deer browsing. Fern and Oregon grape and salal. She hoped she would never have to walk this.

She noted, too, a number of roadways opening into the woods and, slowing the car, saw they led to cabins she hadn't been aware of before.

Here is where Karen had stretched out during an earlier snowfall. Karen. She must do something about, not the girl, but Trudy's own reaction to her presence. She was not going to let Karen spoil her vacation with pay.

"Nor," she informed the steady fall of white, "her attempt to isolate me from any masculine callers. Dr. Whalen and Dr. Kern are fun."

Maybe she would have to out-think Karen. Yet how? She might keep Karen and her mother from Mrs. Morse's room, but, especially if Pamela came up, she could not forbid her the lodge proper. And if there were a man around, Karen would be there.

"If I could learn why she acts as she does," she mused.

Then her mind swung to the young river sailing under

the bridge and, swiftly, to a car on the opposite side of the span, slowing to let her cross first.

"Nurse," a voice called from the car, "the very girl I wanted to see. I have something for you here."

Trudy looked at Dr. Thomas Whalen and bit her tongue before she could say, "Don't hand it to me with your left hand."

"Typewriter," he explained. "I'll meet you in the village at the coffee shop. All right?"

Even the car kicked up its hind tires, Trudy thought. Dr. Whalen could have suggested the garage, post office or store. He hadn't. He'd said, "Coffee shop," and that meant something to her. Thank goodness she'd bought new clothes, a compensation for the ensemble of her student days that he hadn't noticed.

He noticed the grey and gold of this costume and shook his head admiringly. "I think Miz Alpin's in the wrong profession," he remarked. "She should take weary nurses under her motherly wings. You look glowing with health."

Possibly, but Trudy wondered if her cheeks would glow quite as vividly without someone like Dr. Whalen around.

Then he grew sober. "I had a reason for not wanting to go to the lodge," he confessed, and added this was as doctor to nurse. "Yet I wanted you to have the typewriter. Dr. Morse told me why you needed one. He is greatly relieved. He believes this project will offer the therapy his wife needs, isolation from irritants and an interest which will keep her mind, as he said, 'off her conscience.' Though he tells me you made a contribution to that."

"Dr. Morse gives me too much credit," Trudy objected. "I made chance remarks only."

"And that," Whalen's famous smile accompanied his words, "is why they could be accepted. She was braced against any dynamic thrust."

He said he'd better be heading back to Dane. He'd had a trip to make to check a favorite aunt. And when he was discussing her case with Morse, the doctor had asked if he'd deliver the typewriter.

"And you'd better be getting back to the lodge," he added, looking out on falling snow now like a sheet finely woven. "You do have snow tires?" She had.

"This keeps up, we'll have some skiing on Medicine; not have to go over the range."

Trudy told him of her quest for an ancient cook book and dictionary, and he said he knew just the place to find them. He would take her there another time. If she accompanied him, they'd neither one get away before lunch.

Happily she shopped for nonessentials as she waited, then saw him burrow through the snowfall, laughing.

"I wish I had time to wait and watch you figure these out," he confessed. "There are sixty-four pints to a bushel; thirty-two quarts to the same; and four pecks—"

"Easy," Trudy disparaged. "Two cups to a pint, and I take it from there."

She was ready to pull out, Dr. Whalen having gone to his car, when Deputy Sheriff Kline appeared. "Watch your road," he warned. "A white Cadillac ahead of you. Stopped while you and Dr. Tom were having coffee, then drove on."

Trudy thanked him and looked down at her fur-lined storm boots. "And I can always walk, if necessary."

He hesitated a moment, wanting to tell her that by the way Karen had jerked the car, he knew she wasn't pleased at what she had seen. Then he decided, as he told his superior, he "didn't want to act like an old woman."

Besides, he reasoned, even as Trudy reasoned as she drove on, what could Karen do?

Yet she drove even more warily. It was a relief to reach the woods; their great branches meeting overhead were still holding their load of snow, giving better visibility.

Perhaps, she reasoned, something would interpose itself between herself and Karen, giving her better visibility into her dislike. Yet she was quite sure any nurse or any person for that matter who dared interpose herself between the girl and her specific goal, no matter how small, would be considered an enemy.

Suddenly she remembered Dr. Whalen saying he had a reason for not wanting to drive to the Morse Lodge. And she, knowing of his own cabin nearby, had wondered.

He probably knew Karen was due in and felt he'd be detained, she reasoned, for socially he was identified with the Erskine-Pamela-Karen group.

As her car neared the Erskine turn-off, Trudy glanced up and slowed. A large figure, heavy coat over her head, was waving her to a stop.

"You got Dr. Erskine with you?" called the woman, nearing.

"No. Do you need a doctor?"

The woman panted a moment. "Not yet," she gasped, "but the way Miss Overseine's acting, won't be long. He left a note sayin' he'd gone skiing on the Old Slide, wherever that is, and she was fit to be tied. Said he should ought to be there to check on her mother. I'm the new housekeeper. They brought me up from the city to this." And she threw out an explanatory hand.

"How is Mrs. Overseine; how does she appear to be feeling?"

"Plumb tuckered and beggin' her daughter to shut her mouth. 'Side from that, she's hungry."

Trudy couldn't keep a tiny smile from touching her lips. "Then, if advisable, why not give her something to eat, enough to tide her over until the doctor's return? He is most meticulous about keeping appointments."

The woman nodded. "That's how I figured. Thanks." And she turned to lumber up the hill.

Still thoughtful, Trudy drove on to the Morse car shelter, took the typewriter out first and started toward the lodge, naturally looking down for sure footholds.

She could have sworn there had been many taking that same path since snowfall. Oh, but there couldn't have been that many; these were obviously old mud tracks, filled in with fresh snow.

Mrs. Alpin wasn't in the kitchen. Mrs. Alpin, she soon learned, was in the living room, arms akimbo, looking down on the divan which stood before the hearth.

A voice mumbled from there, "I must be arrested immediately. Put her in Dane emergency. *She* must be arrested."

Mrs. Alpin looked at Trudy and shrugged her shoulders. "Is he ever out!" she said.

"He?" Trudy placed the typewriter on a chair and scurried around to look down. Dr. Erskine, or a reasonable facsimile thereof, lay there, feet on pillows, head hanging over the edge where his feet should have been.

"Nurse. Want the nurse," he mumbled.

"I am Nurse Holmes," she assured him.

"Call sheriff. She broke my ankle; then she forced me to ingest poison. Murder," he muttered, stiffened a little and corrected it to: "Homicide."

"Trudy, do something!"

Trudy looked up to find Mrs. Morse leaning against the balcony railing, her cheeks pasty white.

"But what happened?" she asked of Mrs. Alpin.

"Said no half-baked slope man was a goin' t' tell him when he could ski or couldn't. So he took off. After they'd more or less put him together ag'in, they carried him here and dropped him on me. So I set his ankle and snapped his neck; then I give him some easement. He's just come to."

7

SUDDENLY Trudy was all Nurse Holmes, R.N.

"Mrs. Alpin, what did you give him? Of what was it composed?"

The housekeeper sighed dolefully. "Not what I should have. Miz Morse, she put her head over and told me I didn't dare. So I took me the aspirin pills she threw down, two of 'em, dropped them in the hot broth I was fixin' for our lunch and made him drink it down, boilin'."

"And his ankle?" Trudy was looking at one of the neatest bandages she had ever seen.

"Just threw it out. I put it back where it belonged. Neck just a little off center. Back now. Looked his head over. No dents."

Trudy was back, the nurse in her pushed to the background. Dr. Erskine was suffering a trauma of fear. But that was too much under the circumstances.

She made a swift movement for the downstairs telephone and called the sheriff's office. When she turned back to the others, she reported Dr. Whalen would be alerted by the state police motor patrol and would probably return immediately.

Mrs. Alpin motioned her aside. "I just had to," she protested. "I wanted to let that ankle swell to a football, but if I did we'd be stuck with him, 'long with her. She's enough. I didn't do him no harm. I been settin' bones for thirty years, give or take. Live off in the woods like I have, you got to know something."

Trudy took another look at Erskine. He had lapsed

back into peaceful slumber. His respiration was normal. She hurried upstairs and steered Mrs. Morse to her room.

And suddenly they were both overcome with laughter, though, as Mrs. Morse warned, with Erskine it might not be a laughing matter.

"I know," Trudy agreed. "That is why I had the sheriff radio patrol cars to bring Dr. Whalen back. From what I heard him tell Dr. Kern, Mrs. Alpin has worked on him many times.

"Mrs. Morse," she asked suddenly, "was that aspirin you sent down to Mrs. Alpin?"

"One was," her patient replied; "the other was equanol."

Trudy relaxed. The non-barbiturate and the aspirin, coming immediately after relief from the pain of a sprained ankle and probably some neck tendon, had plunged Dr. Erskine into the rest he had been needing ever since she had known him.

Trudy slipped hurriedly into a fresh uniform, even as she talked to Mrs. Morse in the doorway. She told of the Overseines' housekeeper and her quest.

"If we telephone," Mrs. Morse said, "they'll all swarm down. I don't believe Dr. Erskine should have that confusion, do you, Nurse?"

"We'll let—" She paused as the telephone rang, and in a moment Mrs. Morse was back.

"That was the sheriff's office. A patrol car caught Dr. Whalen. He's en route back; should be here, the sheriff says, within the half-hour."

Trudy prepared her patient for needed diversion from earlier excitement. She sat in the chaisette before a glowing hearth fire, a tray with broth and custard at one side, and in her lap a mammoth "White House Cook Book," vintage 1887.

"So you'll know what to do when you become sunburned," Trudy informed her soberly, "use horseradish paste."

"Horseradish! I'd rather be burned by the sun—"

Trudy hurried downstairs to find Dr. Erskine still sleeping peacefully. This both was and wasn't good.

The Nurse on Medicine Mountain 63

Let him awaken before Dr. Whalen arrived, and he, rested and at ease physically, might raise the lodge roof; even call Karen.

In the kitchen, she found Mrs. Alpin, still moody. "Better eat up," she advised. "Goin' t' need your strength. Times not even Tommy can quiet that one down."

Trudy sipped the "lethal" broth and wondered how Erskine could have been so alarmed, then remembered something had been added. Yet it was not enough to cause him alarm. The cause was rather fear of "the witch doctor."

On a pad she made a note of exactly what the housekeeper had done in rendering first aid and knew she could not have done as well. Nor had she, Mrs. Alpin personally, been responsible for the extra fillip to relaxation Mrs. Morse had tossed down; the two pills were of similar shape and also similar in color.

"Regardless of what Dr. Whalen says to Karen," she warned the housekeeper, "we have to be prepared for a visit when they leave. She'll want to know everything. For that matter, so do I. Exactly what happened?"

"Well, like the book says, 'Character is Destiny,' an' if you don't like your Destiny you'd better up and change character. Dr. Erskine doesn't ski too good; not like the other men folk around here. So he up and decided on some quiet practice."

"Quiet?"

"Nobody around to see him do he fall on his face."

"Didn't he know there wasn't enough snow?"

"There's quite a bit over on the slide. Don't melt off there. Sometimes even in June there's drifts. What he didn't know was there's snow and there's snow. Folks on the mountain here hire them a man who does know. He checks the ski area.

"Well, him and a crew was out there when Dr. Erskine showed up. They tried to stop him. They couldn't. They told him there'd been a slide earlier. He could see the big boulders. The little rocks, just covered, he couldn't. He didn't.

"He was out cold, so they brought him to me, like they'd been bringin' themselves, years on end. That's all."

If it only were, thought Trudy. Then she heard a car and hurried out to intercept Dr. Whalen, brief him an outline of the therapy Mrs. Alpin had used.

Dr. Erskine awakened drowsily, greeted Whalen, started to sit up, then remembered. "Get me out of here, Tom," he ordered.

"I will. I'm taking you straight back to Dane. We'll give you X-ray and anything else you and the chief feel necessary."

Now Erskine was remembering even more. "Take that thing off my ankle. I'll be crippled for life."

"I wasn't. I was sixteen when she set a nasty twist for me. Fact is, Miz Alpin has handled more ankles than the two of us and a half-dozen others."

"It doesn't just smell; it stinks!" Erskine stated.

"Doesn't it?" Whalen replied, happily. "But this I'll say. It does take out inflammation."

"Didn't have me time to make up the ones that don't smell," Mrs. Alpin said apologetically. "You know, beat up white of egg—"

"I know. And you put some on his neck, too. Fine; it will wash off. Now, Nurse, about Dr. Erskine's house guests—"

"Oh, lord," groaned Erskine.

"Anything you want from your place? There isn't? Then, Nurse, after we have cleared, give us time to reach the main highway, then telephone and say—" He remained in thought for a moment. "I have it. Tell whoever answers that Dr. Erskine and I are rushing back to Dane on an emergency."

"Yes, Doctor," sighed Trudy in relief. Then she prayed fervently that the thick curtain of falling snow between the Morse and the Erskine lodges would hold until Dr. Erskine was helped to Whalen's car.

It wasn't sight; it was hearing that alerted Karen. She had taken the precaution of sending the housekeeper down to intercept Trudy's car and for a moment was satisfied. Then, when the sound of a second car was heard, she remembered what she had seen at the coffee shop and this time sent Dr. Erskine's "man" down to check on the car.

She decided to give him enough time; then she would march straight in to Mrs. Morse and tell her her nurse was meeting men in the village instead of attending to her patient.

She had started her march when a car labored past the turn-out. She tried to run, slid, landed in a snowbank and arose in wrath. In another moment she was heading back to her own car. She knew snow driving. She would catch up with them and let them know exactly what she thought of them for neglecting the Overseines, sick as her mother was.

Her anger worked out quite well for Trudy. By the time she had called the Erskine Lodge, Karen was on her way, and she could talk to Mrs. Overseine. Mrs. Overseine was not the type to worry over another's emergency and gave Trudy quite a run-down on her own ailments.

Eventually Trudy was able to insert one line of diplomacy. Even as she was ill and needed quiet, it was a great relief to have for a neighbor one who could understand why Trudy needed a "few weeks" without outside stimuli.

"Oh, my, yes." And she was off on another recital. However, Mrs. Alpin had prepared for this and soon was jangling a hand bell so close to the telephone the talker could hear it and accept Trudy's claim she was being called to duty.

"Sure hated to do that," the housekeeper apologized, "but I've heard her before. Don't know when to stop. Feel right sorry for her kind. The more folks keep away from her, the longer she talks when she gets them cornered. Then the more they try to see it don't happen again, the harder she tries to see it does. Downright pitiful."

Maybe, thought Trudy, this accounts for Karen and her drive to escape from or into something.

"What is Mr. Overseine like, or do you know him?" she asked absently.

"Handsome," admitted Mrs. Alpin grudgingly. "Tall, white hair, white moustache, grey eyes. But he's an over-your-head looker."

"A what? Oh."

She had met a few who looked over one's head, as though seeing something they preferred. They were always gracious, yet left one feeling not present, not accepted.

And wouldn't that be maddening to a woman like Mrs. Overseine? Or was he partly responsible for her being what she seemed to be?

"Successful," Mrs. Alpin went on. "Travels a lot, and ain't t' home when he is there."

Trudy, going up to check on her patient, admitted to Mrs. Morse her mind was rapidly developing antelope qualities.

"It has to leap to keep up with Miz Alpin, and I wouldn't miss a word. Each is pertinent."

Mrs. Morse beamed and called her a dear child, and Trudy was able to ask how the other resort people accepted her.

"Some call her eccentric, some a character, but after she's handled a few emergencies they appreciate her—with reservations."

But no, she objected to a remark Trudy made, Mrs. Alpin did not practice folk medicine as a rule; not if she were able to obtain her preferred drugs.

"Here," she handed her the book, "look under Pharmacopoeia."

Obediently Trudy opened the book, her glance catching a line: "Even washing the feet tends greatly to preserve the health."

Wouldn't Dr. Erskine writhe? While Dr. Tom and Dr. Jake would chortle a happy, "Why stop there?"

Then she turned to section indicated to read, "In compiling this part of our hints, we have endeavored to supply that kind of information that is so often wanted in time of need and cannot be obtained when a medical man or druggist is not near."

And they would not have "been near" many people,

The Nurse on Medicine Mountain 67

over a hundred years ago. Even fifty odd years ago, doctors in outlying districts were dependent upon horse and buggy, after having been alerted to crises by a mounted rider. Telephones were yet to become part of normal household equipment.

Then she read a few prescriptions, noting a recurrence of zinc and lead, ammonia and alum. Especially did she note the recurrence of opium, the barbiturate of that day which had grown to be such a scourge.

"Now turn to Domestic Surgery."

Thank goodness she'd had her appendix removed years ago, thought Trudy. However, reading the first section, she found it was devoted to bandaging and contained recurrent warnings to call a doctor, or take the patient to the nearest medico if specific symptoms were noted.

Yet there were detailed directions for caring for minor injuries, and what stalwart man of wood or field of that day would cry doctor?

"Actually," Trudy admitted, "there is a lot of common sense in this for people isolated from professional care. But I doubt any Mrs. Alpin could purchase these drugs across the counter or from a wholesale house without a pharmacist's license."

"And that is where Mrs. Alpin has substituted folk medicine," said Mrs. Morse.

Trudy went to her room, purportedly to relax. She planned to consider what she had just read but couldn't. The snow still fell steadily, though now it seemed less like a curtain and more like a lace veil. And she thought of people, those this case had made important to her.

Especially she considered the three doctors. How thrilling that really for the first time she was meeting them as a person as well as a nurse.

Dr. Erskine. She must learn more of his background, try to find out why he was so rigid.

Suppose Dr. Whalen had not made that call to his aunt? Now how could she have handled such a situation? She feared he would have handled it himself once he had regained a clear head. And heaven help Mrs. Alpin if this had occurred.

Dr. Whalen. Now why had he not wanted to come to the lodge? And having to come, why had he not wanted even to stop at the Erskine Lodge to pick up Erskine's inevitable "bag" and alert the guests or even "the man" he'd brought up? Maybe she'd learn some day.

When Dr. Morse made his usual telephone call that evening, he asked to speak to Trudy. When he was through, she went flying downstairs to the kitchen where Mrs. Alpin was stirring some savory mess.

"What you all lit up about?" she asked.

"My spirits just had an Orange Pekoe rinse," Trudy replied. "Dr. Morse said such nice things about us. And, Miz Alpin, Erskine is actually laughing at himself."

The housekeeper's shoulders relaxed. "Didn't know he had it in him."

"Ankle X-rayed. Amazing, said Dr. Morse. And he feels fine."

She didn't tell Mrs. Alpin Dr. Morse and Whalen had saved him the misery of a stomach pump and the tension of awaiting the findings on a blood test, by telling him the contents of the "poison brew" she had forced on him.

"Hm," Mrs. Alpin brightened, "could be that landing hard on both ends the same time knocked some sense into him."

Trudy was ready to launch into a defense of an associate when a crash sent them both running to the rear door.

Opened, it revealed a tall, thin man arising in sections and, once up, looking down at the snow-blocked staircase and consigning it to a region never associated with snow or cold weather.

He was, he said stiffly, Dr. Erskine's "helper."

"Well, come right along in," Mrs. Alpin greeted him warmly. "Bet you could use yourself a cup of coffee and a piece of pie. What brings you down here?"

He brushed himself off, looked surprised, then

The Nurse on Medicine Mountain   69

pleased, and Trudy deduced he had been led to expect the door slammed in his face rather than this warmth.

"I've come to lead this nurse here back to the other lodge. Mrs. Overseine called Dr. Erskine at the hospital, and he said for her to get Nurse Holmes up there at once, then have her call him."

"Mrs. Overseine is ill?" Trudy brushed the housekeeper back to keep her from exploding.

"Well, no, ma'am, it's the young miss. She took off after Dr. Whalen's car, and her car bogged down and she was stuck, so she tried to walk home. Fell down a few times. All told, she got her clothes right soaked, and she's running a fever, from the looks of her.

"Like she said," he admitted with rare honesty, "if she didn't think she might die of pneumonia if she didn't call on you, she'd next to die without you in preference."

Trudy promptly forgot everything but her profession. "Do you know what Dr. Erskine has at the lodge? Medicine? Thermometer?"

"Well, those things he's got in his car, and his car is stuck in the snow up near the ski area. Can't try to get it out, because he's got the keys in his pocket down in the city."

Trudy gave thought to driving up to Erskine's, then gave it up. With both Dr. Erskine's car and Karen's temporarily immobilized, she had better save hers for an emergency.

Mrs. Morse gave quick though unhappy consent to her leaving and extracted a promise she would telephone back as soon as possible and, if she returned that night, have "the man" return her.

But Trudy, after picking up "the man" twice, decided she'd make a safer return alone.

Karen Overseine was not in bed. She was on a divan before the fire, and for a moment Trudy, blinded by the sudden flame shooting up the chimney, wondered if what she saw was a reflection. Then she decided it was the skin of a wildcat, complete with head and showing its teeth, that she saw.

70   *The Nurse on Medicine Mountain*

"You certainly took your time," Karen greeted her pettishly. "I must not be ill. I can't afford the time. I have invited guests to a mid-week ski party, the only time Dr. Kern has free."

8

MAYBE she hadn't been wrong, Trudy thought as "the man" came in with a glass in which a thermometer was riding. That wildcat on the wall was revealing his hatred no more than the girl on the divan.

She looked away, only to find a cougar literally snarling at her from a side wall; looked down, to find a brown bear showing his incisors.

"Miss Overseine, if you will open your mouth," then hastily, "then keep it shut," for she was trying to talk with the thermometer under her tongue.

Not too bad, she reasoned, checking. A hundred and three. Possibly more temper than temperature, though Karen did seem chilled.

"If you will tell me exactly how you feel, I will relay the information to Dr. Erskine."

"My car," burst from Karen, "simply must be brought up. As soon as you've given me whatever I need, I want you to go after it. That man is utterly useless; he couldn't even bring Dr. Erskine's car back from the ski bowl."

"Without keys, how could he? I can call the village garage. No, Miss Overseine, I am not walking to wherever you left it, then attempting to accomplish what you could not achieve.

"Now if you will answer the questions I place, fine. If not, I am returning to my patient, Mrs. Morse."

And why, she enquired of the wildcat over the fireplace, haven't I a Mrs. Alpin at hand with hot broth into which to drop some quieting capsules?

"Very well, but remember, I intend to listen to your conversation with Dr. Erskine," Karen warned.

"An excellent idea," Trudy agreed. "Then I shall let you talk to him. I want no responsibility for one of your uncooperative temperament."

There were a few sputtered "re-allys." Then Karen subsided and replied to questions, considering each thoughtfully. And as she did so, looking up sideways before she answered, Trudy wondered if she were trying to force some of Dane's younger men up to check.

"May I suggest you weigh your answers if you intend to give that houseparty," she finally sighed. "If you feel as you say you do, an ambulance will be sent up from the city, and you'll be spending your party time in the hospital with someone else acting as hostess."

Karen's symptoms changed instantly.

Trudy was surprised that Dr. Erskine replied immediately. But then she didn't know he was, for a change, occupying a bed at Dane, held for observation not so much for his own welfare as for Mrs. Alpin's. Dr. Morse wanted no repercussions to strike his valuable housekeeper.

"I am speaking from your lodge," Trudy began, "with Miss Overseine on an extension." Erskine couldn't stifle a groan nor Miss Overseine a bit of a snarl. She hadn't known "the man" would signal the nurse.

However, it did give the doctor an excuse to express some crisp truths, to lay the immediate future of the patient right in her own lap.

It was, he stated, too early to give an opinion. He knew Nurse Holmes had to return to Mrs. Morse. If Miss Overseine were interested in a quick recovery, she would go to bed and remain there until Nurse Holmes was free to check again the next morning.

There was, he reported darkly, a virus around. If she showed any indications of having harbored it, she should call off her party or risk infecting everyone and perchance have a lodge filled with some very sick guests.

And then he did groan audibly, and Trudy smiled. What a houseparty that would be, with everyone under one roof but not enjoying it.

The Nurse on Medicine Mountain   73

Trudy then said, "Miss Overseine wishes to talk to you; when she comes on the line I shall hang up." But the crash of a receiver forestalled any conversation between Erskine and Karen.

Erskine said he was phoning a prescription to the village drugstore. He was also sure his keys would reach there in time for "the man" to pick them up and then go after it. Unless she found Miss Overseine worse in the morning after a check-up call, she was to remain with Mrs. Morse.

Trudy turned from the telephone to find the housekeeper and "the man" had been listening and nodding agreement. Miss Overseine, the housekeeper reported, had "gone to bed." She would call when she was ready for the nurse to come up.

"Now, if you will please tell her I must leave in ten minutes to attend to my patient—"

"That gives her five," said the housekeeper happily; and waddled away.

It was six, not five minutes later, that Karen sent word she was ready.

Entering the bedroom, Trudy thought how typical the scene was. Seriously ill patients cared not at all how they looked to one attending them. Those using a minor illness for a purpose tried posture and sound effects.

If they only knew what an irritant this was to doctors and nurses dedicated to alleviating real suffering, Trudy reasoned, they would not strain for effect.

Karen did look ill and injured. Trudy, glancing at the dressing table, found the reason. She had been using a liquid makeup over the bruised eye area and had removed it with night cream.

She refused food of any kind and scorned a citrus drink.

Trudy nodded. "But not taking liquids during a run of temperature does dehydrate one. Can't think of a quicker way of starting wrinkles."

Quietly Trudy offered the simple remedy Erskine had left in his medicine cabinet, then, after a few suggestions, left, reminding Karen she was within telephone call if needed.

The lodge was heated by an oil furnace. "The man" assured her Erskine had had the large tank filled the day before. And there was wood cut to the different lengths of the hearths in nearly every room. As for food, the housekeeper threw up both hands. Plenty, such as it was. Trimmings.

" d Mrs. Overseine?"

T..e daughter had made her go to her room, lest she herself have something "catching."

She had gone willingly and had "et well."

And now Trudy was free to trudge back through the snow to that vacation with pay; that dream world of a deep chair, a glowing hearth and a good book, with a touch of romance somehow slipping in.

"What a day," she breathed, leaving "the man" at the foot of the path he'd laboriously dug from the Erskine Lodge to the road; a path she beieved would be well filled by morning, though now the snowfall was fitful.

"Alone?" cried the indignant Mrs. Alpin as she entered.

"Easier than picking him up," Trudy said absently. "Miz Alpin, I'm so starved I'd eat a wow-wow sundae."

"Got you somethin' better, a full-course personal pie."

En route upstairs to check on Mrs. Morse, Trudy's mind made the leap: personal as in individual. And so it proved, a golden crusted circle in sections; a forerunner of frozen dinners, with even one triangle of wild blackberry pie.

Trudy enjoyed her four-course pie before Mrs. Morse's hearth fire, reporting with considerable restraint, what she had found at the Erskine Lodge.

"I think," she said carefully, "she was tired and frustrated. Then chilled by wet clothing. But I doubt she will have more than a light cold. She's too interested in her forthcoming houseparty."

Mrs. Morse considered this, then asked how she felt

The Nurse on Medicine Mountain 75

about not being included, considering the isolation of the area in which she now lived.

Thoughtfully Trudy replied, "I doubt any nurse expects to be included. Not that she feels socially inferior, but rather that she is on duty, a status which sets her apart; impersonalizes is a good word."

Inwardly she rejoiced. Suppose an invitation had been forced from Karen, what a time that girl would have given her, and before doctors with whom she would have to work in the future!

Both nurse and patient were weary after the excitement of the day and ready to retire early, but Mrs. Alpin put in a final appearance, mug in hand.

"Just sniff," she ordered Trudy. And Trudy, relieved she did not have to sip, drew a deep breath and nearly went over backwards into the fire.

"Didn't say inhale," the housekeeper reproved, hitting her between the shoulders. "Nothin' but pine resin in boiling water. Sure kills any bugs you got in your head; cold bugs, I mean."

And everything else, Trudy would have added. But, having caught her breath, she smiled wanly. "We call it vaporizing. Usually use some menthol compound. But, Miz Alpin, I do believe this is more effective."

Morning found Mrs. Morse still sleeping comfortably, so Trudy slipped downstairs, pondering the sharp hurt with which she had awakened.

She knew it was ridiculous, yet there it was. She could accept Dr. Erskine at Karen's party, even Dr. Whalen. It was the thought of Karen really giving the party to introduce Dr. Jason Lee Kern to her friends that disturbed a nurse who had really no right to question his behavior.

Silently she slipped into a chair at the small table, accepting the cup of coffee Mrs. Alpin placed before her, then sipped, looking out on falling snow. The housekeeper said "it" had stopped for a breather overnight, then had started in again.

She continued talking until Trudy's attention was alerted. "Like I told her, takes more to marry a man than meetin' him."

Trudy held out her cup for a refill and even looked at the plate slipped before her, believing she could enjoy the "blind" egg and crisp sausage.

"Take Tommy. Folks everywhere thought they were sewed up, but when she started pulling the stitches he cut himself loose."

"You mean Dr. Whalen and—" Trudy's eyes were round. So this accounted for his avoidance of Karen. "But, Miz Alpin, I can't picture Dr. Whalen being interested in anyone so—"

"She ain't that way around folks she don't want to hold down. Real charmer when she wants to be. Now eat up lest you took her cold away from her or expect to. Shoulda had you take a cold shower when you got up."

Perish the thought. Trudy rapidly diverted her from her concern about the nurse by leading her to talk of Karen, how she had become intimate with the Morse family and, through them, met the cream of the Dane medical staff.

"Well, it was living nearby that did it. Morses still live in the old mansion he inherited. Right select section. Overseines coulda bought any place, but Karen had gone to the same school as Pamela and figured really to rate; tradition was what counted.

"So Karen got neighborly, and you know Pam. She loves everybody. Figures everybody's as decent as she is."

"And the senior Overseines approved?"

"Father didn't care where they lived. Mother sure don't like that. Hard to keep servants even with an elevator put it. She's scared of the thing and uses the stairs. Said this morning they liked to wear her down to—"

"This morning!" Now Trudy was wide awake.

"Yup. Came falling over to borrow some butter Karen forgot to write down. 'The man' and the housekeeper right up and refused to budge. Savin' their strength for other must-do's, they said. But Karen had to have butter on her toast."

Well, thank goodness for that. It meant she no longer needed the services of Mrs. Morse's nurse.

"Sure do feel sorry for her mother. Needs iron. Give her a shot of my tonic; just extract of bark and some other things. You mark my word. Goin' to come a day we're goin' to get drinkin' water out of a separate faucet. Them health fellows are going to get wise to what we don't get out of this pure water and spike it with minerals."

Fortunately, Mrs. Morse's bell tinkled, and Trudy fled.

She found her patient in such excellent spirits she wondered if Mrs. Alpin were slipping her some "extract of bark and other things."

She was wondering what kind of bark when she heard a new sound and, with Mrs. Morse, went to the north window to see the first snow plough come in, followed by snow mobiles with skiers heading for the bowl.

No more than four feet had fallen around the lodge, but she had been assured this much and more had fallen on the area beyond the summit, insuring safe skiing.

Wistfully she watched, then turned and began counting her own assets: beauty around her, the kindest of patients, an amazing housekeeper. And who knew but that some of Karen's guests—male, that is—might drop in to check Mrs. Morse?

Cheerfully she went about her duties, rejoicing that there was a project under way. Snowed in as they were, nerves could grow taut and healing ground lost.

Trudy practiced her typing and, reassured as to her competence, began copying the notes her patient had made the previous day. And always there were tidbits she shared when, hearing laughter, she would go to the next room.

"Trudy, listen to this. Isn't it priceless?"

And she read: "Early Rising. The difference between rising every morning at six or at eight, in the course of forty years, amounts to twenty-two thousand hours, or three years, one hundred and twenty days."

"Yes, but does it tell how much of those extra years in your life are a gain by telling what time to retire?"

"No. Oh, and here is how to fill a decayed tooth."

The day passed with surprising swiftness, and the skies, as though satisfied they had done their duty, gathered such moisture as was left into puffy bags of scarlet and gold and peach.

"Better take you a hike," warned Mrs. Alpin. "Goin' to freeze solid tonight. Think I'll run down to Tommy's and see did he pack his pipes proper."

Trudy accompanied her and looked a bit wistfully at the cozy interior. She preferred it to Erskine's with its display of hunting trophies, which she doubted had been brought down by his gun, then forgot everything but the sight of Karen's car, returned earlier, heading toward the Morse Lodge. As it neared, Trudy saw Karen at the wheel.

Mrs. Alpin was in the kitchen and Trudy at the door before it slithered to a stop. And if Trudy held to the door a little stiffly, it was because Karen Overseine was waving to her, even calling her, "Trudy" instead of "Nurse."

Warily Trudy went down to the car to have her guest lean from the car window. "Trudy, as I'm *persona non grata* at the lodge, I thought you wouldn't mind sitting in here with me a moment?"

Considering the flushed cheeks and pink nose, the nurse quickly accepted. "You really shouldn't be out in this weather," she reproved Karen.

"I know." She sniffled a little and cleared the huskiness from her throat. "But I had a cabin fever—nerves. I just had to talk to you. I was so rude yesterday, and you were so kind. And I do feel much better because you showed such excellent restraint and took care of me."

Trudy closed her eyes and opened them again. It must be the flamboyant sunset. She had never faced such radiant charm as Karen now turned on her.

Gently she replied, "A person who is ill is not considered accountable, especially when running a temperature."

The Nurse on Medicine Mountain 79

"Forgiven? Oh, wonderful. And really I feel well enough to—" She hesitated, then said brashly—"even enjoy one of Mrs. Alpin's astonishing dishes. No, seriously, our own housekeeper has prepared dinner and I do think I shall dine properly, taste or no taste, now that I'm forgiven."

A little stiffly Trudy said there had been nothing to forgive. Miss Overseine must return to her home, and she would advise retiring early.

"I did want to talk to you about the party, but first I must see if 'the man' who returned Dr. Erskine's car to him has found us the servants we'll need. Well, then, later?"

She also called after Trudy, returning to the house, to give Mrs. Morse her kindest regards.

Mrs. Alpin looked very solemn when Trudy entered, and when she said Miss Overseine had only run down to thank her for attending to her the previous evening, the housekeeper grunted an unintelligible phrase which sounded most peculiar.

Mrs. Morse, too, seemed disturbed by the change in Karen, though she indicated it more by attitude than words. Trudy wondered if Karen had had some ulterior motive in coming down to apologize.

She telephoned the next morning. "The man" had found a "brace of help" and was driving them out in the family station wagon.

"Trudy," Karen then said with a note of pleading in her voice, "could you come up on your afternoon walk? I have to prove to Dr. Erskine I'm not 'contagious.' Besides, I do want to talk to you."

Mrs. Morse acceded to Karen's request, "though the doctor did not expect you to take on extra duties," she protested.

Trudy said it wouldn't take long, and shortly after lunch set forth on a day of shining gold sun on snow which caused her willingly to accept the dark glasses Mrs. Alpin had brought forth.

Karen met her at the door, and again neither mother nor housekeeper were in sight. Like a docile lamb, she submitted to the nurse's ministrations and nodded when Trudy said her temperature was nearly back to normal.

"Then do have coffee with me." And Trudy was led around to the divan, facing the fire and the snarling wildcat.

"Trudy, when your off time allows you to join the party, I wonder if you would do something for me. I was counting on Pamela, but she is not coming up because 'Erskie' is on duty."

Now Trudy waited. What could she do that Pamela would have done?

"The five-day forecast isn't pleasant. My guests are going to be lodge-bound and will grow restless. I must have something to entertain them, so I thought of that ridiculous book of Mrs. Alpin's. You'll slip it away from her somehow. I know you can; she thinks so much of you.

"We'll read it aloud. Some of the contents are really a riot."

9

TRUDY looked up. No, it was the wildcat, not Karen, that was showing its teeth. Or was it? Karen was talking on blithely, unaware of Trudy's silence.

"I managed to copy this one the time I had my hands on that priceless book. Listen," and from her pocket she drew a slip of paper.

"Whoever puts up a bath in a house already built must be guided by circumstance; but it will always be proper to place it as near the kitchen fireplace as possible, because from thence it may be heated or at least have its temperature preserved."

The lilting voice went on, then stopped, and Karen looked to Trudy for approval.

"That shows evidence of wisdom and forethought, does it not?" Trudy commented quietly. "Take this lodge, or even a one-floored dwelling. If it were not heated by an oil or even a wood furnace, and not wired for electricity so a heater could take over, and if the bath water had to be carried from fireplace to tub, I doubt many would take more than sponge baths in weather like this.

"Our forefathers were amazingly adaptable, weren't they?"

Here it came, that "Well, really!" And then, "You mean you don't see the humor in this?"

"I did at first," Trudy smiled at her. "Then I thought of the hundreds of men and women carrying water from a spring or a well and later a hand pump, and wondered if I'd have enough strength of character to remain under such circumstances.

"After that I could laugh, but with understanding, not ridicule."

"Hmm," buzzed Karen doubtfully. "But you will find some way of bringing me the book?"

Trudy shook her head and glanced at her watch. "I must go back. It's time for my patient's two o'clock. No, Miss Overseine, if Mrs. Alpin won't hand you the book freely—"

"You must know what she thinks of me."

"That isn't the point. I wouldn't want even a chosen friend to take from me something I treasured without my consent."

Trudy walked to the door without escort, let herself out and for a moment stood blinking. She had thought she had seen a dark figure skirting the other lodge. Probably it had been only a bough loosening its weight of snow; she donned her glasses.

Slowly, she walked down to the other lodge, thoughts halting, even stumbling. Karen planned her coups in advance, even as she had planned her lease of the Erskine Lodge. Knowing she had shown her true colors to Nurse Holmes, she had first tried to offset Trudy's distrust by her charm.

"If she hadn't been pushed for time," Trudy reasoned, "who knows to what lengths she would have gone to win me over? And because of the way her own mind works, she couldn't conceive of another refusing, after having been unconsciously bribed."

She left her boots in the rear porch closet and went in through the kitchen. Mrs. Alpin, head bowed over a newspaper, looked up and nodded.

"Showed her colors," she said with satisfaction after one searching glance. "Save you a lot of trouble."

Witch, thought Trudy affectionately, and continued on upstairs.

Mrs. Morse sat in a windowed embrasure, low tables nearby strewn with paper, some half covering the book.

How far, she wondered, should she go to protect that

The Nurse on Medicine Mountain   83

volume from Karen? How much tell her patient? And what was its intrinsic value, if anything?

Soberly she walked over, lifted the book and, aware her patient was watching her, asked, "How much is this book really worth? Oh, not in money, but—"

Mrs. Morse was equally sober. "I have been evaluating it as I've read and copied. Like Dr. Whalen, I don't know if the medicines and the therapy would have any value to modern man other than their emotional value.

"I mean by that," she said hastily, "it gives readers inner assurance something is being done for their welfare. This automatically reduces fear. With the fear diminished, nature has a better chance to make use of its built-in curatives.

"We're learning more and more about emotional response. I viewed the last Red Cross disaster car, and was amazed to find in it kits of makeup for women, shaving creams, razors and after-shave lotions for men."

Trudy nodded. "Even cards of safety pins. The attendant called them 'more builders.'"

Mrs. Morse observed, "As a nation, we've had a scourge of disasters within the last few years. Whole areas were cut off, despite air-lifts. As this was written when men and particularly women did not have access to drugstores and supermarkets, it could see them through; above all, give assurance others had lived for a lifetime on simples.

"But why, Trudy? Is the book in danger?"

"It could be," murmured Trudy.

"Then how fortunate we were forewarned; now we shall take better care of it. And," she smiled at the nurse, "it will give fresh impetus to my project."

Trudy's whole torso slumped in relaxation. She had been braced against that silly old book being stolen and perhaps carelessly lost by Karen—if it were a silly old book. For weren't all or most simple books of other days looked upon as ridiculous?

There were exceptions. Dickens, derided in his day, had outlived the literati of his era.

At least she had worried unnecessarily and had been

able to reveal there was a threat to the book without voicing any accusations.

Now let Karen have her houseparty.

Even let her have Dr. Kern. If he were one to be fooled by synthetic charm, he deserved her.

Synthetic charm. Her thoughts whirled around the phrase, reducing Nurse Gertrude Holmes to a new low. For hadn't she planned, as soon as she was released from this case, to purchase some of that commodity?

"Mrs. Morse," Trudy asked, "what does the book say about Charm?"

A check of the index showed nothing. "I imagine in those days they gave it the original connotation; a spell cast by magicians; a form of hypnosis." Then she smiled. "One wonders if it is different these days.

"Imagine, for instance," she continued innocently, "some man charmed into marrying a girl, then awakening from the spell."

"Hmm," agreed Trudy, "what a 'morning after'! Could be a girl would have a better chance of enduring happiness if she settled for being the best of her natural type."

Dr. Morse drove in that evening and, after checking on his wife and being quietly briefed by his housekeeper, beamed on the nurse.

"I congratulate myself," he informed her. "I wanted the best of everything for Mrs. Morse, and that's exactly what I chose. I hope I can make this up to you in some way."

"You have," she assured him. For hadn't he just confirmed her deduction? "And this is such a change."

The three had dinner downstairs, a festive occasion.

Morse decided his wife might make daily trips to the main floor and, if she felt equal to it, slow trips back up, with many pauses.

A momentary cloud passed over Trudy's face when he said they would turn the one downstairs guest room into a small office for his wife. The inner lodge doors had no locks; just bolts on the inside.

Then he switched her attention with small talk of

Dane Memorial, commending Trudy for her efficient handling of Erskine.

He spoke of Pamela. "Mother, I suggest you tell Pam you are writing a book, but not describe what type. If questioned, merely say a professional never discusses subject matter and that you are taking a professional attitude toward this."

Mrs. Alpin was serving what Trudy was to decide was the most delicious pudding she'd ever eaten, when Dr. Morse observed that Dr. Jake would be able to spend only a few hours at the party. He would appreciate Mrs. Alpin checking on Tom's cabin, drying bedding if needed.

"A command performance?" Mrs. Morse inquired. He nodded, and Trudy thought: here again Karen had tried to maneuver rather than to gain wholehearted assent.

"What," Trudy asked the housekeeper later, "did you put into that pudding?"

"Eight eggs, six ounces of butter, two lemons, juice an' rind, powdered sugar," droned the woman, "pastry linin'. Then it got seasoned with words. Sure feel sorry for that girl."

By now the nurse was adept at keeping up with Mrs. Alpin. "Why?" she asked.

"Got everything and nothing. Don't know as much as she thinks she knows, an' acts ornery. But," she sighed, "can't nobody tell her nothing."

Then she announced she was going out to build up her calves, and Trudy had better come along. Tomorrow a body'd have to wade through snow, the ski road being occupied by weekenders and their guests.

It was a beautiful evening with enough of the bronze afterglow to light the scene, touch the snow hills, darken the pine and fir and cedar.

An adventurous star poked its nose through the thinning veil and Trudy lifted her head. "The air even smells good"—she stopped, then added, "I think."

"That there's the sulphur springs you got you a whiff of," comforted Mrs. Alpin. "Nothing better to get the poison out of your system. Sweats out, mostly."

Trudy declined a trip up to the cave which held the springs but watched Mrs. Alpin go, pulling a small flashlight from one pocket, a flask from another.

She was remembering something she had read about sulphur intake, heavy perspiration that colored the sheets and drove the unwary from close proximity to the patient who had taken the diaphoretic.

By the time they returned to the lodge Trudy knew what Mrs. Alpin had meant about "building up her calves." Her own ached to the point where a hot tub was welcome, though this was not "near the kitchen fireplace."

Dr. Morse left early the next morning. He would stop at Mrs. Alpin's village home and talk to her husband about arranging the office on the first floor.

Trudy waited with considerable interest for the man's arrival.

He was exactly what she had anticipated, a big, easy-going man who teased his wife unmercifully and brought a glow of pleasure to her cheeks, especially when he told her eating at the town café was spoiling him. Then he added, "For some of your cooking."

"I think," Trudy told Mrs. Morse later, "that it isn't love which is the prime ingredient for a successful marriage, but a sense of humor."

Mrs. Morse agreed, then sobered, and Trudy suddenly realized that she had never found this in Dr. Erskine.

Her own felt slightly dehydrated as the day wore on. The road to the ski bowl was one parade of happy people going or returning from zestful exercise.

And then, on the hill above, something new was added. What she had thought merely a sharp slope curving around the Erskine lodge turned into a toboggan slide. And look at Karen! That figure at the top must be she, in pale gold this time, arms waving, indicating which girl would ride with which man.

Which man was Dr. Kern?

Well, she'd walk the other way; she didn't have to expose her aloneness to the party. And she could have been one of them, she reminded herself, had she been willing to sell a portion of her own integrity.

Slowly she walked downhill, hidden from the Erskine Lodge party by the Morse Lodge, then by the trees. Here was the creek, one of the tributaries feeding the small river between Medicine Mountain and the settlement.

She found a rounded boulder from which the snow had melted and settled down, trying to immerse herself in the beauty of the scene: the lacy filigree of black leafless alder branches against the yellow afternoon sky; the dark water, white-lipped on meeting opposition, running between snow banks.

And such peculiar boulders! That one down there looked exactly like a woman, a woman with a flask in her hand. A second look, and she saw it was a bottle. A secret imbiber?

Suddenly the figure dropped the bottle and scurried into the low hung arms of a conifer, and a moment later the dark shape was going on up the hill.

Curious, Trudy walked over and glanced down at the bottle and nearly laughed. It was a well advertised mouth wash. She lifted it gingerly and nodded. But surely she hadn't been drinking the stuff. Perhaps she had been imbibing something else and had tried to clear the evidence from her breath.

Now just who around this particular area would feel that was necessary? And should she or shouldn't she discuss this with Mrs. Alpin?

"No," she decided, "that would be an invasion of that woman's privacy, and I'd be no more than a gossip-monger."

Then all thought of the woman flew. Coming down the path towards her was Dr. Kern, in the wildest plaid mackinaw she had ever seen.

"Oh, there you are," he called out. "Been looking for you. Karen said she'd invited you up to the lodge, but she hadn't seen you. We're about to have an ice break, she called it—in lieu of coffee, I presume. Tables look tempting."

"Not to me, after one of Mrs. Alpin's special-special's," Trudy evaded. For why had Karen sent for her? Above all, why had she sent Dr. Kern, if she had.

"Were you especially delegated to produce me?" she asked.

"To be truthful, no." He smiled at her. "I asked about you, said you should have a little fun with your duty, and she ordered some girl to come down after you. But I thought I'd have a better chance of convincing you. You know, doctor orders nurse?"

"And nurse reminds doctor she is on a case?"

"Ah, solution. Doctor shall inquire of patient if nurse is free. Come on; beat you to the lodge."

They arrived together, but it took Mr. Alpin to pick them up. They had struck a stretch of ice on the last lap, and lost what equilibrium they had in laughter.

"Told you the air up here was an intoxicant," observed the housekeeper, looking on happily.

Briefly memory of the woman in the woods returned, then vanished, for Mrs. Alpin was continuing, "Doctor, you're here just in time to give my man a hand. Movin' Mrs. Morse downstairs. No, tain't she needs lifting, but her desk does. Nurse here can look after her patient."

Willingly Trudy complied. Here was her excuse ready made, one Dr. Kern could accept. And wouldn't Karen prefer her absence to her presence, especially under these circumstances, after Kern had insisted upon coming after her?

He remained quite a little while as they pushed the desk here and there to obtain the best lighting, then arranged easy chairs nearby, and a small bookcase with volumes for such research as Mrs. Morse would do.

And then he sank into one of the chairs and admitted, after the day he'd had on the mountain, he wouldn't mind remaining right there.

"What's for dinner?" he asked Mrs. Alpin.

"Bein's my man's here, first-watch stew, he being a seafarin' man 'riginally. Deep dish apple pie for dessert, with whipped cup topping."

For a moment the doctor looked like a boy just home from camp, wistfully considering some of Mother's

The Nurse on Medicine Mountain 89

cooking. Then he stood up and said briskly he had to return to the other lodge.

"I'll take you down a pot so's you can eat after you come in, or for breakfast maybe?"

"And can I borrow coffee for the same?"

Doctor and housekeeper exchanged understanding glances, and he went out.

"Bet he'da ruther stayed here," remarked Mrs. Alpin, and Trudy agreed silently, again wondering if Karen's method was satisfactory. Well, she did win out, she reminded herself. Had she not, she wouldn't have been giving the party at Erskine's.

A wind from out of somewhere caught some clouds napping and drove them across the sky. Trudy, awakening the next morning, found everything about the landscape gloomy. There was no car down at Dr. Whalen's cabin, and a quietness about the Morse lodge, with no prospects of visits within the near future.

It snowed again that night and the next day, and someone from the village telephoned to say the houseparty was breaking up; a few of the guests were seeking transportation out.

Trudy, on her late walk, automatically glanced up the hill at the sound of a motor roaring. She saw Karen's car shoot out of the driveway, heading for the village, and decided she was in one of her arrogant moods. For she blared at another car which had the right of way until the driver eased into a drift to let her pass.

With darkness, Trudy tried to make a book, a fire, and thoughts of a contented patient compensate for some lack she was feeling, but failed. Perhaps Mrs. Alpin could cheer her up.

A car drove in as she went down to the kitchen, and in a few moments Deputy Sheriff Kline entered, his features serious, his voice concerned.

"Mrs. Alpin," he asked of the housekeeper, "are you practicing medicine on city people without a license?"

"Now, son, you know better. Why?"

"Sheriff had a call from the city, from Mr. Overseine's lawyer. They claim that you have been giving

Mrs. Overseine something toxic which is affecting her brain."

"Didn't know she had one," mused the housekeeper, while Kline and Trudy looked at her in shock.

10

SWIFTLY Trudy went to the housekeeper, then turned to Kline. "They'd not send you here to warn her if they were sure of their claim."

"Right. They sent me here to check on Mrs. Alpin until Mr. Overseine can come up and bring his wife under control. Seems she went a little wild this afternoon. She came up from down this way, her daughter said, smelling like a drugstore.

"Miss Overseine asked some questions, and her mother slapped her face and said if she were as strong as she planned to be, she'd upend her and slap elsewhere. Now we all know Mrs. Overseine is a very quiet—"

"Cowed," put in Mrs. Alpin.

"Cowed. I mean quiet little woman, not given to outbreaks like this. Besides, others with her daughter said there was a most peculiar odor about her, and the housekeeper said her clothes and linens—"

"You say she slapped Miss Karen's face?" interposed Mrs. Alpin. "Take back what I said about her having no brains. She has, finally. Hope 'tain't too late."

"Then you have been giving her a tonic?" Kline dangled the bait.

"Only thing I ever give her was a piece of my mind. A big piece. She took it."

Trudy's memory was sweeping down to the figure she had seen from the Erskine Lodge, a figure she'd taken for a wind-swept tree, though there had been no wind. And then later, she recalled, she had seen the boulder that turned into a woman with a flask in her hand that had contained mouth wash.

"Miz Alpin," she pleaded, "is Mrs. Overseine a 'secret drinker'?"

Happily the housekeeper replied, "She sure is. And what she's been drinkin's right hard to keep secret. I got me some here." And she went into the closet, to return with the flask Trudy had seen her fill at the sulphur springs.

"Mrs. Overseine read her a feature story in a Sunday newspaper magazine section, all about how a tribe of Indians living hereabouts, use to bring their young braves up in the spring to drink up and get the cowardice out of their systems.

"Worked out fine, and they went out killing like all get-out.

"Now she didn't want to kill nobody, but she sure did want to stand up to the two that were making her life such misery. So she come to me to ask would it kill her, and how much of the spring water a body should take. I told her the least I figured she'd be satisfied with."

She had turned to draw the coffeepot forward as she finished her recital. Now she made another turn, disappeared into a pantry and returned with a pie.

And then she waited expectantly, and as one, Kline and Trudy burst into laughter.

Something had worked: the sulphur, her faith in it or, Trudy thought, sheer desperation, willingness to try anything, no matter how bitter, to change the life she had been living. But would this, could it endure?

They had finished their repast when a commanding rap sounded at the kitchen door. Without awaiting an answer, the visitor opened the door, and an equally commanding man strode in, a woman trying to keep up with him.

Mr. Overseine Trudy knew; he had fire in his eyes and arrogance in his stance.

Trudy looked at Karen's mother, seeing her for the first time. She was quite short, but had an uplifted chin and defiance in her eye.

"I demand to know what you have been giving my wife." Overseine said to Mrs. Alpin.

"Ain't been givin' her nothing but talk."

"Then you have told her how to prepare one of your dangerous brews."

Mrs. Alpin looked at Mrs. Overseine. "Wisht I had. Looks better 'n I've ever seen her. Got her some color and some zip. Don't look dragged out and crushed down by folks what don't care nothin' about her."

"Where is Mrs. Morse? I shall discuss this with her."

Swiftly Trudy stepped before him. "Not without Dr. Morse's consent," she said. "You may telephone him from this extension. I assume you remember she is here purportedly out of the way of intrusion."

"Karl," Mrs. Overseine was now standing between them, "I told you Malda knew nothing of this. Nor am I taking a brew Mrs. Alpin concocted. She refused to give me anything.

"Furthermore, if you cause any more trouble, I shall walk out of your life, giving the newspapers the kind of story they will spread all over their front pages."

"You wouldn't dare!"

"What have I to lose? I have money of my own. Or I had. I can ask for an accounting."

Overseine turned to the only man present. "Now you can see for yourself. Out of her mind. Should be committed. An Overseine committed."

Panic swept over his wife's face, then she looked at the housekeeper and then at the deputy sheriff. "Those two are capable of having me committed quietly."

"Not with me as a witness," observed a voice, and Mrs. Morse stepped in. "I couldn't help overhearing and came down. Mr. Overseine, you will send down an overnight bag for your wife. Mercedes, you will be much better off here for a few days. It's all right, Nurse—less disturbing than having to worry about her."

Later, she would tell Trudy that, had Mrs. Overseine returned to her husband and daughter at that time, she would have succumbed to their stronger personalities, as reaction from her defiance swept in.

"I think," she looked back once, "the doctor can come out tomorrow sometime. He will set your mind at ease, Mr. Overseine. Nurse?"

With some reluctance Trudy accompanied them. Then, realizing Mrs. Alpin could handle the situation, rid the lodge of Mr. Overseine, better than she, she went on.

There were times within the next hour when Trudy felt she was clearing away the debris from a gradually disintegrating structure, perchance a weak wall which had given way and could cause the fall of others.

Yet would that be a loss? Karen as she was, caused more trouble for more people than anyone Trudy had ever met.

"Mrs. Alpin said—" Mrs. Overseine looked up from the pillow Trudy had tucked under her head—"that we harmed people more than we helped them when we gave in to their whims. What do you think?"

"I think that you are the only one who can answer that," Trudy told her, "because only you have been permitted to watch the effect."

"Then she is right, and now I must—"

"Have a bite to eat and then a good night's rest. Tomorrow the confusion of today will be cleared away and you can reach a wiser decision."

"I still feel I was right. Karen was so furious at Dr. Kern for preferring to spend his time with you, she was planning another party, you included. When she let me know what she was going to do, I slapped her, hard. The housekeeper held her, or she would have struck me. But it's true. Both Dr. Whalen and Dr. Kern prefer—"

"I imagine both of the doctors are so accustomed to having nurses around they don't see the individual; just an image of someone who accepts them as they are. Now open."

She "opened," swallowed, then opened again. "And I told her she'd never win a husband her way. And she told me to look at the marriage I'd had, doing it my way. And that's when I made up my mind to leave them both, because she was right."

The Nurse on Medicine Mountain

Fortunately, Mrs. Alpin came in with a tray and Mrs. Morse, behind her, was ready for a second tray which would divert the new patient from her own woes until the capsule had taken effect and food was ingested.

Trudy went to her room to stand at her window and look out on the gloomy night. The snow seemed more gray than white. Kern and Whalen had preferred her company? Or had they both preferred that little cabin, its solitude and quiet, so the cacophony of the crowds around Karen?

Karen would assume any man would gravitate to a younger woman, and she, Trudy, was the only one near the cabin.

And what had Karen planned for her? Trudy wished she dared ask Karen's mother. Whatever it was, if Karen continued to run true to form, it would land back in her lap.

It wasn't necessary to call Dr. Morse. Mr. Overseine had called immediately upon returning to his lodge, and now the doctor wanted to talk to the nurse privately.

"Trudy, you did your stretch in the mental ward. What is your opinion of Mrs. Overseine?"

She protested she had not talked to the woman enough to establish any opinion. If he wanted merely her reaction, she could offer that. Pressed, she replied, "I'd say she is on the very ragged edge, and if she is not relieved of the irritants, she could go over. She's balanced enough to know what has caused it and has made an effort to correct it. It is possible if she were given medical and psychiatric treatment, she could enjoy life for—"

"Yes, go on." And when Trudy wouldn't, he laughed and said he understood. And now he would talk to his wife.

Trudy, making her final evening check, found Mrs. Morse surprisingly calm.

"I believe what has happened is good," she explained. "Now they will all have a chance for happiness, it they accept it. That is up to them. At last Mercedes can start living."

No, the doctor wasn't coming up. Mr. Overseine, he thought, would drive his wife to Dane Memorial the next day.

She hoped Trudy wouldn't mind if they had Thanksgiving dinner on Sunday. Dr. Morse would be free and would bring Pamela up with him. Pamela would attend some Thursday dinner with Dr. Erskine.

Mrs. Morse offered one last observation. In asking a nurse Trudy's age to Medicine Mountain, he had feared she might become bored. At least she hadn't been that.

But after Thanksgiving, a different type of activity would begin. With the ski patrol in the bowl, families would come up more often, and there would be color on the hillsides if not at the lodge. And now, of course, they would lift the ban on Pamela. She might bring a friend or two on her trips up.

Trudy carried a last tray of cups and glasses down to the kitchen, to find Mrs. Alpin subdued.

"Sure do feel sorry for her," she commented.

"She'll be all right. She's sleeping, and tomorrow—"

"Not her; her daughter. She's the one that's got hurt by her mother. No, no, not today; all along, since she was a little tyke. Saw how her mother give in to anything just to keep peace. Didn't like what she saw, so she went all out the opposite way. Mother let her get by with it, because her father didn't want to be bothered and she didn't have gumption enough to stand up to him."

"You mean it would have made a better person of Karen had she lived in a home where her parents literally fought?"

"Didn't say fight; said, 'stand up to.' Difference. If a person thinks things through to a right answer, then they don't have to fight; they just stand steady."

"Which means you don't blame Mr. Overseine?"

"Don't matter how pretty a dishrag is; if it's all slumped down wet, nobody's goin' to love it."

Trudy couldn't quite see anyone loving a dishrag,

but caught the housekeeper's meaning and had to agree.

In her room, she considered Karen and admitted she did feel, not pity, but rather compassion. Karen didn't "think things through." She sought desperately for a goal, such as a man and marriage, then headed for that goal, destroying anything that impeded her journey, only to find goals could fall before an onslaught.

Opening her window, Trudy breathed deeply and then laughed. At least she had learned how this mountain had won its name. From young Indians who, without benefit of refrigeration or canning, met spring with lassitude and came to the springs to clear poisons from their systems.

"I remember Mother telling how her great-grandmother started spring with sulphur and molasses—sulphur to clear the system, and molasses to give needed iron."

Thanksgiving-Sunday dinner proved quiet. Trudy had her first opportunity to become acquainted with Pamela. The girl was lovely, spirited and gracious and truly beautiful.

She asked Trudy if she felt she should take up nursing while waiting for "Erskie" to get established in his profession; if she thought she, Pamela, would make him a better wife.

"I don't know," Trudy replied honestly. "Look at your mother. I doubt if a physician could have a more satisfactory home life."

"That's what I told Karen," Pamela commented. "If I were a doctor, I'd be glad to have someone who knew nothing about my profession."

Trudy winced. Then valiantly she recovered. "I imagine it is the person, not the profession, which determines a man's choice."

Karen telephoned, then drove down, refused to come in and instead had Pamela come out to her car, where she seemed to be talking earnestly.

A totally different Pamela returned from her half-hour with Karen. There was an arrogant tilt to her chin, a condescension in her manner, and Trudy could sympathize with the Morses. Karen's influence seemed to destroy more than just those within her own family.

"Alpy dear," she began, "I want to copy one of those delightful squibs from your book."

"Which one?" Mrs. Alpin looked at Trudy and caught her involuntary warning.

"Why, that—now let's see. I think it was—" She floundered.

"'When the hand is clean it needs no screen'?" suggested the housekeeper.

"Yes, yes, that's it."

"I'll write it down for you." And grabbing a pad, she scribbled away.

Pamela, defeated, went to her parents and soon drove off with her father. Mrs. Alpin, watching, shook her head.

"Times I wonder does she love Dr. Erskine, or has Karen told her she should ought to. Can't figure out how a girl like her can give in to a one like Karen."

"I doubt Karen ever shows the side she's shown us to her," Trudy suggested.

"Well," Mrs. Alpin sighed, "Dr. Morse's holding out for a delay till he gets established, and Dr. Erskine isn't about to get the chief down on him. Maybe time will straighten it out."

Time, thought Trudy rather desperately during the next few days. She, who had longed to have little to do, was having just that. She gave thanks for the project she had inadvertently given Mrs. Morse. It also helped her. It blotted out hours with typing.

Dr. Morse reported an epidemic in the city; two or three, for that matter. It was the unseasonable weather; it kept Dane Memorial filled with extra beds in the halls and every medical man on the run. Trudy felt a momentary envy of her fellow nurses.

Morse also reported on Mrs. Overseine, calling her by telephone "our neighbor." She had embarked on a South American cruise, with a psychiatric nurse as a companion. Her husband seemed quite cheerful and definitely surprised at a certain physician's findings.

For several nights the lights blazed at the Erskine

The Nurse on Medicine Mountain 99

Lodge; then suddenly the big building was dark and there were no signs of life anywhere.

Days later, Trudy, driving Mrs. Alpin to the village to "load up on account of a hunch," learned the reason from Deputy Sheriff Kline, who invited her to stop with him for coffee.

"Don't know whether it was the mistress or the servants that suffered an acute attack of cabin fever, but it was the servants that packed up and demanded 'the man' drive them back to the city. She followed, intent upon hiring a fresh crew."

They talked about the weather, and he said, as Mrs. Alpin said on the drive back, he'd never seen so much snow so early.

Trudy couldn't judge. She did find driving difficult, despite the twice daily cleaning of scoopmobiles. Then, too, it gave one a trapped feeling to drive that narrow lane with no view on either side and only the dark rasp of snow-laden boughs overhead in the wooded sections.

She had managed a tiny laugh as she'd driven across the bridge. It had creaked, groaned and rumbled, and Mrs. Alpin had sworn it was suffering from rheumatism. "It's that old. Makes a body want to tuck it in under blankets to heat it."

Following Mrs. Alpin's advice, she blanketed her own car with carriage robes the housekeeper brought down from the lodge, then patted its fenders and told it she'd freeze to it if she tried to "bank it up."

Intent upon a blazing fire and bowls of the soup Mrs. Alpin had left simmering, Trudy, nearing the lodge, stopped short. The housekeeper was coming around the side, prodding a wheelbarrow before her.

"Want to give me a hand?" she asked. "Got to unload tonight. Mrs. Morse called down the three young doctors are comin' out. Epidemic's about over."

Unload, after the cartons they'd carried up? And the doctors were coming? Surely the sun had come out. But no, the skies were darkening.

At the car, Mrs. Alpin opened the luggage compartment, and Trudy saw hundred-pound sacks of something.

"Three kinds o' beans," enumerated the housekeeper, "taters an' split peas. That there's a sack of ham hocks. That's onions—"

"But, Miz Alpin, the doctors couldn't eat that much in months."

Soberly the woman nodded her head. "Bought up 'fore I heard they was coming. It's just a feelin' I got in my bones. They ache."

And Trudy wondered if the housekeeper would be the next to need psychiatric care.

11

SHE'D take emergency ward duty any day in preference to this, Trudy thought after they'd loaded the barrow and pushed and pulled it up to the rear, then used a garden cart to wheel the commodities on inside.

And why had Mrs. Alpin wanted to hurry before the arrival of Dr. Whalen and Dr. Kern? They would have helped. Then Trudy nodded. Dr. Erskine would have looked down his nose, and just try to explain to that man she had stocked up on dry groceries because her bones ached.

There was another reason for the hurry. Trudy was really concerned when Mrs. Alpin gave it. The doctors wouldn't be up until "way late," after she and the others were bedded down, and they'd go directly to Whalen's cabin to sleep. She was only going to cook for them.

"These sacks," she told Trudy seriously, "just don't hold water. That's why I want them in tonight."

Trudy worried that one all through the hot soup she'd been awaiting. Of course snow was water, yet—

"Now, then, see here—" Mrs. Alpin came in from the storage room, rubbing her hands. "Could feed an army, given cause."

Trudy considered discussing the housekeeper's vagaries with her patient, then decided against it. Mrs. Morse was making truly remarkable strides toward recovery. She was up and downstairs several times a day and ventured outside occasionally. Work on the book absorbed her other hours, hours that dragged for her nurse.

"She'll be ready to return home the first of the year, easily," Trudy reasoned this night, then glanced at the calendar. Was she herself ready to end this vacation with pay so soon?

She'd have to start planning projects for herself. She'd find a new apartment; she could afford a better one now. She'd join something, she didn't know what, and learn how to fill her off duty hours with gay companions, a luxury she hadn't been able to afford.

Only now she didn't care. Now the future looked exactly like the landscape: one dull pattern of monotony.

Suddenly lights built up in the Erskine Lodge starting with the lower entrance. Floor by floor, they sprang into golden oblongs. Wouldn't Karen return when Whalen, Kern and Erskine were due?

No sense in brooding; she'd go down to the kitchen.

She arrived to hear the radio blaring. "Hear that?" came from Mrs. Alpin in triumph.

Trudy heard something about a "warm air mass moving south from Canada" At the moment she'd welcome it as a change from the penetrating chill.

"Cold's having its big time tonight. Tomorrow, who knows? That's what my bones are tellin' me. Joints just screamin': Get ready for rain."

"Oh," muttered Trudy. Regardless of the prophetic powers of Mrs. Alpin's structural extremities, a belief it would rain accounted for the movement of the sacks to shelter.

"Bones," Mrs. Alpin informed her seriously, "are smarter than brains. Stone Age men and Indians didn't have them no forecasters, so they listened to their elders who'd been livin' through weather. They told them how to read their feelings."

She continued, and Trudy didn't bother to tell her modern man and his "bones" lived differently. Their "caves" were heated, as were their means of convey-

The Nurse on Medicine Mountain   103

ance from office to home. Nor was their diet restricted to what was immediately available.

Above all, she thought, they had modern medical advice at hand should the weather creep up on them and wreak havoc.

Trudy slept fitfully that night, believing her ears were attuned both to the arrival of the three doctors and the arrival of Mrs. Alpin's rain.

Only the doctors arrived. When she made her first trip down, Whalen was wailing, "Corn snow," and Erskine was gloating, "What better excuse for me to stay off that ankle." Kern was just coming in with a mammoth log.

They greeted her jovially. Even Erskine, perhaps infected by the good fellowship of the others, said, "Still wearing your balloon tires." That left her puzzled until Kern, returning from the other room, brushing moss from his sleeves, explained.

Trudy looked at Erskine with such approval he visibly relaxed. "There have been times," she said darkly, "when I'd have welcomed them, wouldn't you?" Now she knew why Kern had been laughing that long ago day at Dane.

She was to breakfast with them, they insisted, on hot cakes; each man would carry his own stack. Again Erskine bridged a gap. "Seeing what her cooking has done for you, I can hope."

He really wasn't so bad, once one got under that hard-shelled exterior.

They made tentative plans for the day, though Erskine asked why they bothered. Karen was "in residence" with a lot of their friends. She would have every minute charted.

"I am here to rest," Whalen said stonily; "not to jump to the crack of anyone's whip. Each of us has had as tough a three weeks as we've ever had. We owe it—"

"To our patients—" the other two droned.

Erskine turned to Trudy suddenly. "Are you going up?"

"I have work here," she evaded.

Dr. Kern studied her a moment. "If I were to ask you as a special favor, would you?"

"Uninvited?" Trudy flashed.

"But Miss Overseine told me she had tried previously, and asked my assistance."

Onto the table was slapped a platter of hot cakes, and into the air came the brisk voice of the housekeeper. " 'When Fortune smiles she oft designs the most mischief.' " And away she sailed.

"I have heard her called Miss Fortune," intoned Whalen, and Kern bristled.

"You are all being unfair."

Trudy stood up. "If you will excuse me, I see my patient is ready for me." And she blessed Mrs. Morse for coming out on the balcony at that moment.

But she didn't travel swiftly enough to escape Kern's defensive, "No, I am not falling for her. I am thinking of our nurse. Morse gave me a run-down on her life. She's never had an opportunity to mix with her own kind."

Mrs. Morse closed the door behind them. "These dear men, brilliant in their own field and blind in the social world. In short, Nurse, doctors are human. That is why they need wives of intelligence."

A moment later she mused, "I wonder how long before Karen has all three up there. As soon as they leave, I am going down to lock up my writing room for the duration. I am having one of Miz Alpin's hunches."

Trudy's sigh of relief must have been audible, for Mrs. Morse laughed lightly. "I do not miss too much, Trudy," she said softly. "And if you wonder at our willingness to let Pamela be at Karen's beck and call, it is deliberate. Pamela is not stupid. She might resent our calling her attention to Karen's faults but if she sees them for herself—"

Pamela gave some indication she had seen something when she arrived with the two friends who would stay at the Morse Lodge. She would, she admitted, prefer to remain there.

Three girls and three men. Trudy was ready to re-

The Nurse on Medicine Mountain 105

tire into the impersonal shell of her uniform, just when she had thought life might offer some gaiety. But these girls were different from the others she had seen around Karen.

In no time they had surrounded her, plying her with questions, listening enviously to her answers.

"You are really doing something with your life," one explained their interest. "Well, one thing: I intend to tell Father I am going to become a nurse's aide, regardless of his objections."

"I won Dad over by telling him how much better I could care for my own family."

Mrs. Alpin appeared just then to signal Trudy. "Telephone," she announced with such distaste Trudy knew who was at the other end of the line.

Walking away, she heard the girl complete her sentence, "I start right after the first of the year," not knowing it would have any further meaning to her.

"Nurse," Karen was brisk, "the doctors think Ruth Anne may be coming down with this new virus. They are not yet sure, but need someone here to look after her. Naturally, I can't ask a guest or any of the help to expose themselves to contagion, but you, being a nurse, would know how to care for yourself."

"Miss Overseine," Trudy's voice was cool, "I am on a case. I can't leave it without the permission of the attending physician."

"Then start packing. I intend to call Dr. Morse."

Trudy turned from the telephone to relate what Karen wanted, and Mrs. Alpin nodded. "That's how she got the doctors up there. How come they didn't call?"

"Probably because they knew protocol."

"Humph," grunted the housekeeper. "Now I can't ask you to call up there and find are the men or aren't they comin' down to lunch."

They were. They literally steamed in. Kern came immediately to Trudy and asked if she had any occasion to have "flu shots." She hadn't. Then she was not to go near the other lodge. There was no sane reason Karen couldn't have the girl driven back to town, except that Karen would have to rearrange her plans for the day.

Whalen went to the telephone to call the girl's parents while Erskine simply sat holding his head, bemoaning the fact he had let them in for this by leasing the lodge.

Pamela, hearing voices, came to the kitchen to cry, "Erskie, you mean you didn't know? And you leased it? You didn't just offer it to her for—"

It was Whalen, through telephoning, who took her by the shoulders and gave them a small shake. "After being around Karen as long as you have, don't you know how she works? This time it was through realtors. One called Erskie, offering two thousand for the lodge up to the first of the year. Any young doctor just starting out isn't going to refuse that, not when he had no need of the place, having my cabin for an emergency."

Pamela turned to the other two girls who had followed her, "I don't know how you feel, but I am not going skiing with Karen's party today."

"You nor nobody else," intoned Mrs. Alpin happily. "Moderated after midnight. Temp's dropped forty degrees since I got up at six o'clock. Look outside."

All turned. A wind had sprung up, and rain was just beginning to fall. "Nothin' like having smart joints," stated the housekeeper. "Now you run along in, and I'll whip up some lunch in nothing flat."

They all offered to help, and she said the biggest help they could be would be to be "out from underfoot."

She even waved Trudy in with the others, and Trudy took that route to go on to Mrs. Morse.

Someone turned on a radio, and on her way upstairs Trudy heard a program interruption, a weather warning. A vicious storm was riding in from the Pacific with gale winds, some reported on the coast at seventy miles. Heavy rains were forecast in all areas. Motorists were urged to stay off streets and roads or risk being hit by falling trees and poles.

Poor Karen, thought Trudy; even the weather is

against her. Imagine trying to keep her party entertained with no outside activity.

She looked down to find Dr. Kern gazing up at her, his face a mask of worry. Then she understood. If no one arrived to take the girl with the virus to some other place, it would be she, Trudy, who would have to do what she could. And how could anyone drive safely in this storm?

Then her spirits soared to match the wind singing its paean of triumph around the lodge walls. He actually cared what could happen to her.

Trudy and Mrs. Morse went down to lunch with the others, a "pick and choose" affair which Mrs. Alpin disdained to call a buffet. Never had she felt so at ease with any group, and again her spirits lifted. She was not a complete social loss.

They discussed the storm, at times having to talk above its fury, though its maximum strength was still hours away.

They also discussed influenza, now no longer a single disease but labeled alphabetically by categories and almost impossible to diagnose by type until it was well under way.

Treatment was also restricted. Erskine had chanced to have tetracycline with him. He'd given this to Pamela's guest. From now on, about all anyone could do was watch her temperature, ease the headache and, if it turned to stomachic distress, pray they had on hand something to ease and check the inflammation.

Care and total rest were, they agreed, most important.

A blast struck the lodge and, had it not been built of mighty logs, would have shaken it.

"Something tells me the girl is not being called for tonight," observed Erskine, then turned to the others. "And something else tells me we'd better set off for the village and go into a huddle with the druggist; see what he has on hand we might need if any of the rest of the party—"

"And something tells me we'd better be prepared to

walk," Whalen interposed. "See what that blast did to the car shelter. It will take us hours to lift the roof."

Trudy offered her car, but after consultation they decided they needed one in case of a later emergency. Right now they couldn't be sure some tree would decide to fall as they drove past.

"We'll have a better chance walking," they said. And they added that it would give them the exercise they needed. Did Mrs. Alpin need anything from the village they could bring back?

Nothing, she replied smugly. But she had something they needed: slickers and souwesters and, if "their feet fit," rubber boots.

Watching them set off, laughing at each other, Pamela expressed some worry.

"Needn't," the housekeeper reassured her, "A tree's a sporting thing. It cracks like a pistol when it breaks, then howls a dirge on the way down. Plenty o' warning."

The three didn't know what to do with themselves until Mrs. Alpin suggested they come to the kitchen and give her "a few hands." Her bones seemed to be reporting again. She intended to "bake up." They'd never learn any younger.

Half an hour later, a furious Karen telephoned. She had received word cars were being turned back, and her guest who was ill would not be moved to her home or a hospital. Nor would she tolerate having her there, infecting everyone else.

"I'll call you as soon as I have talked to Mrs. Morse," Trudy told her.

This time she spared Karen nothing.

"I know Ruth Anne," Mrs. Morse mused. "She's the type who couldn't tolerate being treated as a leper. Karen's attitude is more debilitating than the germ."

"If you don't need me and if there is any place I can take her—"

There was the one room to the left of the kitchen stairway. It had its own bath and was more or less isolated.

"Then—"

The Nurse on Medicine Mountain 109

Mrs. Morse nodded, and Trudy, donning her own rain clothes, went on out to her car.

It seemed a little ridiculous to be talked to from a distance, after she had reached the Erskine Lodge, but no one seemed willing to assist her get Ruth Anne to the waiting car.

Trudy used laughter in lieu of assistance. She said she wanted her near so she could look after her and that Mrs. Morse was happy to have her in the one guest room which was not occupied.

A second trip for her clothes, and Trudy wondered if Karen would burn everything in the room after they left.

Mrs. Alpin was waiting when they drove as near the rear door of the lodge as possible. The three girls were on the porch, crying, "Welcome home, Ruth Anne," and onto Trudy's shoulder poured tears.

"They really don't mind," the sick girl said.

A warm room, a warm bed and welcome. Ruth Anne slid her aching body into its comfort, accepting a cup from Mrs. Alpin and acepting her words, "This'll have you up and kickin' in no time."

Trudy turned too late. "What did you give her?" she demanded.

"Nothin' but a bit of chicken broth and a sop."

Sop as in soporific?

It was too late to do anything now. Trudy turned to the upper hall telephone extension to call the girl's parents and to reassure them that their daughter was at the Morse Lodge with three physicians and a trained nurse in attendance.

Belatedly she realized she had placed herself beyond the pale of comradeship with the others. Yet she could not have done otherwise.

"Better get you some wood up," Mrs. Alpin commented, and nodded at the small Franklin stove in the room. "I got me a hunch."

Trudy frowned, then remembered this room, an afterthought, was heated by electricity, the pipes from the oil furnace not extending this far.

"Hunch?" Trudy echoed, and stopped. Below them

in the big room was darkness. The radio, to which the girls had been listening, had stopped. A power shortage, and for how long?

A moment later three weary young men tromped in.

"We couldn't reach the village," was the tenor of their report. "The old bridge has gone out, been washed downstream."

12

TRAINED as they were to conceal any fearful condition, the three doctors could not suppress the undertone of excitement in their clinical observations on what they had seen.

The river had risen to the turn-off. The only reason they knew the bridge was gone and not submerged was that they had caught sight of it, rapidly breaking up, lodged against a great stand of trees downstream.

The north side of the village was inundated, the low-lying summer cottages having been placed there by people wanting to be near the stream. Fortunately, not too many were in residence at this time.

They could see trucks backed to the homes not yet struck, see people milling around.

"Won't they worry about us over here?" Pamela asked.

"We're the lucky ones," Erskine told her, "and they will know it. The county men know we're not threatened by high water. They'll know we have oil and wood to keep us comfortable."

"Might be a good idea to check our bags," offered Whalen. "If we're short anything we might need in an emergency, we could telephone and have it dropped by 'copter. I have a hunch the whirly-birds will be out in full force."

Mrs. Alpin, bringing coffee to the returned men, said, "I figure the power lines are down, an' the telephone lines will be."

They were. Perversely, this had a more devastating

effect upon the party than the loss of electric power. Swiftly each tried to reassure the other.

"It isn't everyone," Mrs. Morse soothed them, "who has a corps of medicos in residence during a disaster."

Mrs. Alpin, having considered all things, decided it was time for the party to realize how fortunate they were in comparison with the rest of that part of the country.

"I got me a whole brace of gadgets for my transistors," she told them. "Here's the big one; you listen in. I'll keep my little one in the kitchen. Figure if you tune to the two disaster stations, you'll get the most news."

"Isn't she wonderful?" demanded one of Pamela's guests. "She even had us help with the baking this morning. We're really loaded with bread and pies and —well, other things." She wasn't quite sure of the names of the odd dishes that were tucked in beside the familiar ones.

Trudy returned to Ruth Anne, remarking happily how lucky they were to have spoken to her parents before the lines went down. "Good omen," she said, "if there are such things. Now they won't have to worry and you worry about their worrying."

"I'm only worrying about Karen," the girl whispered huskily, "and the way she treated me. I couldn't believe it. I still can't. I know when I'm better I'll be furious."

"I doubt it. You'll realize, instead, that she needs our understanding, our pity. You said you had pet cats. When do they turn on you?"

"Oh! Nurse, I never thought of that."

"So now you rest. Have a nice nap."

Trudy hurried to use the last of the daylight to bring in wood for the night. She came in with one swing carrier, to be stopped by three angry young men. Why was she wasting her strength with them around?

She smiled after they had left. They were truly on a different basis now.

"What on earth is that gosh-awful smell?" Erskine asked irritably after leaving his armload and motioning Trudy outside.

"Pitch," she replied truthfully.

Whalen, stepping out after him, nodded gravely even as his eyes danced. Then he raised his brows at Trudy, and she smiled.

"How did you know it was pitch?" Erskine had made another trip in, glanced at a small tin on the narrow ledge of the heater, discounted it and returned.

"Because I was jolted back on my heels the day I went up to attend Miss Overseine."

"A preventative?" Whalen asked. "Good ...inking on her part, especially when we've nothing to take its place." He turned to Erskine. "In lieu of vaporizers. Resin rather than a camphor derivative."

And Erskine's shoulders slumped in defeat.

Dr. Kern appeared on his second trip with, not wood, but a folding chaisette, a pad and two throw rugs. In a moment he had turned that short ell of the balcony into a private rest room, the rugs over the balcony railing shutting off the view of the big room below without closing off the warm air rising from the hearth.

"I have an idea the nurse will need rest," he informed the others. "We three will rotate. I'd say each should take full duty, but—"

"That's been worrying me, too," Whalen picked his thought out of the air. "It might be a good idea to go scouting after daylight."

"How many have been trapped here on the side of the bridge?" Erskine asked. "Any way of learning?"

"News travels fast in a small area," Whalen said. "Word will get around there are doctors here, as well as Mrs. Alpin. Stop bristling, Erskie. Where she is, there's food."

A mighty blast struck the lodge, and they stood holding their breath, wondering if it would succumb at some weak point, and wondering more what it could be doing to other less stable structures.

"Think I'd better take a chance and hike up to my place when there's a lull. May spend the night there. That crowd could be in a state of advanced hysteria by now."

Urged, Dr. Erskine remained for dinner, and, as

the other two would remain in the Morse Lodge, set up a flashlight code signal. Until ten o'clock, he would signal on the hour: up and down for all right; a tilt if something seemed to be brewing; and back and forth if he needed help. "Then you two can draw straws," he sighed.

Trudy, coming out after checking on her patient, found a tray table set up, a deck chair before it. On top was a vast platter with macaroni, cheese and tomatoes and a dish of sliced onions.

Topping the raw onions was a note, "Eat them all. Nothin' better for scaring germs out of your throat."

After a moment's exasperation, Trudy remembered her grandmother telling about the ever-present pot of onions stewing in honey during winter, to be used as a cough syrup and preventative. At that, they tasted rather good, as did the huckleberry muffins.

From below came a hush, then the radio giving news, the summation of the storm's destruction insofar as it was known. With telephone lines down and the movement of traffic at a minimum, few details about outlying districts could be included.

The storm, the weather caster came on to report, should die down by midnight, but more rain was forecast. As soon as air transportation was feasible, planes and 'copters would make an aerial survey. People in isolated areas needing help should arrange some type of signals. They were warned to make no requests unless it was vitally necessary, lest they deprive others in desperate need.

"That lets us out," gloomed Erskine. "I think Ruth Anne is better. By the time we signaled and medicine was rushed in—"

Trudy, looking at her patient, had to concur. The girl was resting more easily; her labored breathing had softened.

Yet it was a night to remember. Whalen took the early shift, checking on the hour for Erskine's signal. Trudy was relieved it was he and not one of the other two who was present when Mrs. Alpin appeared with a small flat sack.

The Nurse on Medicine Mountain

"Made it light," she informed them gravely. "But them lungs of hers needs stirrin' up so she'll rid them of the poison."

"The contents?" demanded Whalen.

"Flour of mustard, flaxseed meal and some lard. Not too much mustard. Feared she'd burn."

Whalen tested it by putting finger to tongue, let out a slight yelp, then concurred about its use.

"Can't hurt her," he explained to Trudy, "and it may help."

He told her she'd better rest while she could, and she complied. Nature had an unhappy habit of hitting ebb tide in the early morning hours.

Even as the storm was waning, so was Trudy's strength, and she welcomed Kern's thoughtfulness in preparing a chaisette.

It was he who awakened her, a cup of coffee in hand. Ruth Anne's fever had broken early; she was ready for a dry gown and bedding.

When Ruth Anne was again asleep, this time restfully, and Trudy had used precious hot water to shower and change, she found Dr. Kern waiting.

"Trudy," he was forgetting the "nurse," "you said something about Karen being ill, earlier. I believe you went up to check on her." And when she nodded, "This evening Pamela told me Ruth Anne had not wanted to come up. She'd been having what she called a splitting headache and was running a temperature.

"Now I am concerned. Karen insisted she be present, even as she demanded the other girls join the houseparty. I'm wondering if possible infection couldn't have started among them all before the party began."

"But she seemed much better the next day."

"The fluctuating type. I'm not sure about her physical condition yesterday. There was no doubt about her emotions. Brittle. Then her treatment of the patient in there—"

"And the others?"

He didn't know.

Trudy realized he feared each guest at the other lodge had been exposed to the virus. Caught as they were without access to medicines, a small epidemic could be dangerous.

"Some day," she told him earnestly, "some bright scientist will isolate some radar component which will trace germs, catch them before they strike. Meanwhile, we have Mrs. Alpin."

She waited for his derision, but none came. "If there is illness and we can't get help from the outside, I'm willing to investigate her preventatives. They could be no more than placebos. But relieving fear is sometimes half the cure."

Perhaps this wasn't the dream she'd had, thought Trudy as they sat on the gallery and looked down on a smoky room, a down-draft having sent clouds into the house. Yet they were on a more informal basis than they could have reached at Dane Memorial.

They talked of the days when the book was written, and Dr. Kern said he'd like to study the book, the pages of prescriptions. Perhaps they were the forerunners of much of present-day medicine. It would be interesting to find out.

Twice Trudy roused Ruth Anne, once for a citrus drink, the next time for broth which Ruth Anne murmured was "delicious."

The first outside call for help came before dawn. It was directed to Mrs. Alpin, already in the kitchen stirring vast vats of oatmeal.

"Save the milk for the kids," she ordered Pamela, who joined Trudy. "Sprinkle dry milk on the mush; that'll do. I got us a hundred-pound sack of it the other day."

She set off with an anxious father, and before she returned a man vibrating with indignation arrived. He had stopped at the other lodge to ask for food and medicine and been turned away, the door slammed to his face.

He and his wife, he explained, had come up for the day and been caught by the flood. They were in a friend's cabin, but the windows had blown out on the southwest side, and the cabin wasn't stocked with groceries. He could take it, but his wife was becoming ill.

The Nurse on Medicine Mountain 117

Dr. Kern took Trudy's car, the better to carry sheets of insulating board they had planned to use on Whalen's cabin. These would cover the broken windows. The man was willing to "scrounge" for firewood, but a bundle of pitch kindling was tucked in.

There were a loaf of bread and some cheese for immediate use; coffee and dry milk and sugar; a generous bucket of Mrs. Alpin's dry peas, a ham hock and some onions for later-in-the day rations.

"Oh," Pamela sped after him, "and here's a bit of lard. Once when we ran out of butter, she fried the bread and seasoned it with salt. It wasn't bad at all."

Two other persons called asking for food before Mrs. Alpin returned, and the consultation in the kitchen grew serious.

"I think she foresaw something like this," Trudy told them. "That's why she stocked up. But I think we should hold off until she returns; she may have other and better ideas."

She had. The real Mrs. Alpin appeared, a little grim, determined, but capable.

"Made me a survey. A good hundred caught this side o' the river. Don't know how long before we get calls from the other side. Merchant knows me, and he knows how I bought.

"Now you three girls—"

"I don't have to remain with the patient," Trudy began.

"Need you where there's sickness and folks that is hurt. A sight of them got under trees and wind-tossed roofs at the wrong time. Now then, you three girls get out those wash boilers in the big closet. They're clean. I keep 'em scoured. Then you make up, 'cording to the recipes I got here."

She'd been saving pails, buckets and large tins ever since the Morses had come to Medicine Mountain, though she had a "sight of them at home."

The girls were to dole out beans, with a "touch" of ham hock and one onion to each serving.

"Better than giving them raw food," she stated. "Some haven't stoves and some haven't brains," was her explanation, intimating the uninitiated would not know how to prepare dried legumes regardless of written directions. For, she continued, this being a world of instant cooking women got impatient.

With the first cold light of dawn, Erskine came down from his lodge, bewildered. Utter chaos reigned up there, he reported. The servants Miss Overseine had brought up had gone on strike. They were remaining in their quarters, except when they sneaked out for food. What, they reasoned, was a salary worth if they were dead before they received it?

"Someone else showing symptoms?" Kern asked.

"I'm about to be converted to psychosomatics," he informed them. "I admit I can't diagnose properly with the hysteria up there. But what has me bothered is the number of people being turned away. Do any of you know anything about law?"

A voice said, "I do," and without stopping to identify the voice, he posed his question.

"If I return the full fee for the occupancy of my dwelling, have I the right to take it over and turn it into a temporary hospital?"

Someone mentioned "invasion of privacy" and someone else "right of tenure." Then the one voice said, "Make a citizen's arrest of the party for some violation, and you can take over."

Erskine groaned. What violation? Nothing had been harmed that he had seen, nothing but sick and frightened people who had come for help and been turned away.

Whalen, being nudged from the rear, spoke up. "Erskie, at the time you signed that lease, was there anything in it to allow you occupancy in an emergency?"

"Why, yes, there was. Not that I wanted it; the lessee had that clause inserted. I believe it also included my friends."

"Fine. Then what are we waiting for?"

Mrs. Alpin came forward. "Dr. Jake, you go with him. I need Tommy for a man who stopped a roof with his neck. Him and Trudy," she qualified.

The Nurse on Medicine Mountain   119

Dr. Whalen teased Mrs. Alpin as they started out in Trudy's car again. Was she about to admit there was something she couldn't handle?

"If folks would let me buy my medicine at the drugstore like I used to do, no," she flashed. "But now you got regulations. Besides," she sighed, "there's something about a neck—bein' so close t' the brain—an' this fellow needs all the brains he started out with."

Once outside in the greying morning, Trudy was shocked. The mountainside looked as through some giant hand with talon-like fingernails had scratched and scrabbled, leaving bare the areas of beauty, now a haystack of fallen trees.

One glance downhill, and she found the stream she had once thought beautiful, now a roiling mass of mud and debris, swirling among the trees where she had sat to admire it.

The lodge they eventually reached was quite imposing, and there Trudy learned why Mrs. Alpin had given up. The occupant, equally imposing in his own mind, had refused her further services after the emergency treatment she had given him.

Time stopped, insofar as time might be considered a succession of minutes into hours. They went from lodge to cabin to lodge.

Treatment was given, using the contents of the old leather handbag Mrs. Alpin carried. But somehow, with Dr. Whalen gravely dispensing, it was accepted and visible improvement evidenced.

Each place was cheered by the news there was food available, and that there were tools, especially nails, to repair, temporarily at least, areas devastated by the wind. They and their families could be assured of warmth and sustenance.

"Food," muttered Whalen as they started back toward the Morse lodge late that afternoon. "Have you had any, Trudy, or you, Miz Alpin?"

Suddenly Trudy was weak from the lack of anything since the macaroni and cheese of the previous evening.

"Got me some special things stashed away," Mrs.

Alpin said happily. "Figure we all deserve them." Then she stopped.

Pamela had flown down from the rear door. "Tom, Trudy, Karen is desperately ill and calling for you. You must get up there immediately."

13

TRUDY looked up at the Morse Lodge, already smudged by the early twilight. Up there was warmth, the soft cheer of kerosene lamps and food—Mrs. Alpin's food.

And up on the other hill was the Erskine Lodge, with Dr. Jason Lee Kern and Dr. Erskine and Karen; Karen, who might be desperately ill but was still willful enough to destroy the great, budding hope in Trudy's heart.

"Why should I," Dr. Whalen was asking harshly, "with Kern and Erskine there? Why me?"

Trudy turned to him and said softly, "Don't you know? Don't you really know why Karen acts as she does?"

Mrs. Alpin snorted a little and started off. Trudy talked softly until Whalen said, "How blind I've been! Come on."

Erskine met them at the door, no longer brisk and efficient but looking drained of everything but a determination to keep going until the last demand had been made upon him.

The big room of the lodge was now a ward. Hides with glaring eyes and white teeth had been removed. Cots, chaisettes that had once graced the terrace and the guest rooms, held patients.

"The poor devils," Erskine commiserated, "tried to do things and did everything wrong. Got soaking wet and had no place to dry out. Quite a few had come over to the ski bowl and had no quarters on this side.

"I've done what I could, but—"

"Fine." Whalen spoke cheerily. "I found some replacements. Now you take a rest, and I'll prepare adequate doses for each. I assume you kept charts."

He had.

"But first, let's see to Karen. I am worried about her."

"Let me go first," Trudy begged. "I think I know something."

Wearily she went up to the room she had visited before. And there lay Karen, cheeks scarlet, eyes like those of the trophy wild life that had earlier hung on the walls.

"I thought you'd never get here." Her voice was husky and a bit breathless.

"Well, I am here, and Dr. Whalen is waiting below stairs. Karen, can you understand me clearly? Karen, you don't have to be afraid any more."

"Afraid!" The girl reared up in her bed.

"Your life has been pretty much of a nightmare, hasn't it?" Trudy went on. "When you were small, your mother was petite and pretty, and then—"

"She's a hag. I've done everything within my power to make her see, but she couldn't. And I swore by all—" She stopped and stared at Trudy.

"You swore; you also manipulated. And every time you planned to outwit someone, you did. But the results were not what you wanted. In the long run, you lost.

"And the more you lost, the greater grew your fear."

"Fear? I've never been afraid."

"Fear isn't being afraid. Fear is a sickness, an emotional apprehension that lives with you. That's why you fought so hard. You couldn't bear living with what you felt you had to do because it never came out right. But, Karen, you don't have to fight. You already have everything."

She was listening. Trudy talked on softly until she sank back, her eyes enormous, and within them an awakening awareness.

The Nurse on Medicine Mountain 123

"Dr. Whalen is downstairs," Trudy concluded. "Let him know you know what you've been doing and why."

"If I know." The girl was broken now. "Trudy, tell me more. I've thought these things, but I was afraid to let go. I had to fight, fight—"

Completely drained, Trudy eventually made her way back downstairs to find Dr. Kern standing there looking at her with condemnation in his eyes.

"For a nurse, for a person supposed to have more than average knowledge about the proper care and—"

"Oh, shut up," said Trudy.

"What did you say?"

Trudy looked at him and wondered what she had said. "I think," she made a pretense of a reply, "if just one more person starts telling me what I should or shouldn't do, I shall—"

"What?" he asked with interest.

"Fold in the middle," she decided. "I've had no food all day. I have had only such rest as comes while riding in a car from case to case. You know how much sleep I had last night?"

"Great goodness, Trudy, that is what I am trying to tell you. Who do you think you are—Mrs. Alpin?"

"Askin' for me?" came the voice of the Morses' housekeeper. "That girl needs a pick-up. Tommy, where's my satchel?"

"Here," said a voice, and a man pulled himself painfully, inch by inch, from a chaisette. "She can have my bed. She took care of my kids, you know."

Mrs. Alpin took over. Trudy found herself led away, to the kitchen, naturally, where the now aroused and willing servants were attempting to make up for their dereliction.

Trudy had a vague memory of food being thrust at her, of men in white jackets (she could learn Mrs. Morse had dug out some belonging to her husband) which didn't fit thrusting such things as thermometers at her.

Me and my vacation with pay, she thought when her mind was clear enough to think.

And then she floated down to the Morse lodge and

somehow up to her old room. One of Pamela's friends, the one who intended to become a nurse's aide, had taken over the check calls on Ruth Anne.

Here was a deep, easy chair, a blazing hearth, a huge back log promising embers when the flames died down. Now who had brought that up?

A snore ripped the peace of the night. Trudy sat up. Over there, across the hearth from her, a man was stretched full length in another reclining chair.

Quietly a dejected Trudy slipped downstairs to find Mrs. Alpin alone, checking supplies.

"What," Trudy asked, "did you put in that drink you gave me at Erskine's last night?"

"Call it a drop of courage. Why?"

"I told Dr. Kern, of all persons, to shut up."

Mrs. Alpin hesitated a moment, then posed another question. "Why?"

"I am not sure. I was so tired of being talked down to. I realized I could become another Mrs. Overseine. I'd just spent half an hour telling Karen where she had gone wrong, and then the whole thing hit me suddenly. And I didn't want it. An extreme, I mean—neither Karen's nor her mother's."

Wisely the housekeeper nodded. "'Tain' what a body has got but how she got it. Some work things one way, some the other. But you got to have things come smooth and natural or they won't last."

"What was in that pill you made me take on the drive up?"

"Tonic and stimulant, 999," quoted Mrs. Alpin. "Extract of bark, powdered gum arabic, syrup of marshmallow, syrup of tolu and—"

"Give me another, quick. I must apologize to Dr. Kern. I need extra strength for that."

"Don't figure you have any call to do that," the woman mused, having recognized the figure hovering at the door. "You just slip up to your room and fix yourself pretty."

"Pretty!" groaned Trudy, after one look in the kitchen mirror, which, being made of faulty glass, gave her the appearance of a piebald mule. "Besides, Dr. Kern

The Nurse on Medicine Mountain 125

is having some much needed rest in my living room and—"

Another pounding at the door, and Trudy, with no thought of how she did or didn't look, grabbed the first coat she found and, with Mrs. Alpin and her bag at her heels, took off.

Kern caught up with them as they stepped into Karen's car, Erskine at the wheel, Whalen beside him.

"Am I glad to see you and your bag!" Erskine said earnestly to Mrs. Alpin. "The ski patrol holed in at their shelter. Thought they could sit this out. Then the flu struck. Now they are all down. The least seriously affected made his way down to the lodge."

"Oh, and, Alpy," Whalen spoke affectionately, "Karen wants to borrow the book. Now stop bristling; she needs it. She wants to read what it has to say on the treatment of husbands."

"Hints to Wives," quoted Mrs. Alpin, "197." And off she went, pausing for occasional laughter.

" 'Let him alone until he is inclined to talk; take up your book or needlework (pleasantly, cheerfully) and wait until he is inclined to be sociable. Don't ever let him find a shirt button missing. A shirt button being off a collar or wrist band has frequently produced the first hurricane in a married life.' "

Two days later, Trudy, her own car having been delivered to the ski bowl, rode out, with Dr. Jason Lee Kern beside her. With her car had come fresh uniforms, her own cape and other very necessary so-called incidentals, such as Mrs. Alpin's "shine for your hair."

Probably goose grease in steeped tea, she had thought, but she had used it.

As the car topped the rise looking down the south side of Medicine Mountain, Dr. Kern braked, then parked and turned off the motor.

A whirly-bird was overhead, vast crates in the crane's grappling hooks gradually being let down to a cleared area.

"Line men managed to run a telephone cable over,"

Kern reported. "That will be the first load of food and medicine. But, Trudy, what if there had been no Mrs. Alpin and no book? Not that the book is the answer. We've made a greater advance in medicine this last century than in thousands of years before, yet—"

"The principle is the same? Dr. Jake, I wonder what the medicos of even a hundred years from now will think of our medicines and therapies of today. Can't you hear an Erskine of that era scoffing at our most advanced remedies of today?"

"An Erskie scorning a twentieth century treatise until he is faced with a primitive situation, such as being cut off from the necessities of life."

"Primitive, hmm. But will there be any wilderness areas then, at our present rate of population explosion?"

"You should read science fiction. Then we'll assume, an Erskie and his most brilliant medicos, a Whalen, a Kern and a Nurse Trudy, will be left on some strange planet with a host of sickening earth beings like themselves."

"And a Miz Alpin with a book that has answers?"

"Just so there's a Nurse Trudy around, they'll establish a record."

The 'copter pilot set his whirly-bird down on his home port, puzzled. The only life he'd found on Medicine Mountain had been contained in a car. Two people. A man and a nurse, judging from her cap and cape, though the cap did get knocked off, he thought. He couldn't get a clearer view nor set the 'copter down for a rescue. But then, most nurses knew how to take care of themselves.

Trudy did. When Dr. Jake said they wouldn't waste time like Erskie, who was trying to make a big show before he married Pamela, Trudy quickly agreed.

"I'm afraid some other medico will assign you to a permanent case within his home. You know, Trudy, you've been special to me since the very first moment I saw you."

"That was the Medicine Mountain air and Miz Alpin's tea."

"You hadn't met Miz Alpin or been to Medicine Mountain. You were in the corridor of Dane."

"And my hair looked, as Erskie said, neither this nor that?"

"I didn't notice your hair; just something about you. I didn't make a diagnosis; I—"

The Dane Memorial Staff sighed and/or brightened. Three wedding presents within a month were a strain on the budget. But the change in Dr. Erskine was worth it. And imagine Trudy catching a man like the handsome Dr. Kern.

"All I have to say," remarked one to the group at the table, "is that I'm concentrating on receiving a call to Medicine Mountain."

Mrs. Alpin, receiving a relayed report of this, smiled. "The book says letting things come naturally does more than maneuvering and hard labor."